What readers are saying about *Isis Erotica*

"Fifty Shades of Grey? Even better. Isis rules in 50 shades of color!"
Ann – Los Osos CA

"...a gem of a collection about a woman who will never be satisfied by just one man, although Isis does love them all with great intensity. She has great taste too - these men are to die for."
Kayla – London

"Steamy...Sandra's created a new genre for the sexy intelligent woman."
Barb – Toronto ON

"If Isis doesn't scorch your pants off, she'll levitate you out of them."
Len – Chicago IL

"Wow! Sexy Indiana Jones-like adventure through Las Vegas and Ancient Egypt."
Patricia – Las Vegas NV

"Sex! Adventure! Mystery! Egyptian culture and history! A hot read."
Leslie – Ann Arbor MI

"The Wynn – Whew! Gimme a cigarette!"
Joan – Fresno CA

"Isis is an instant turn-on. Galloping narrative with hot sex."
Mike – Wichita KS

"Isis sizzles. It had me squirming in my plane seat."
Suzanne – Boston MA

"I kept reading certain parts over and over and over again. :)"
Suzette - Paso Robles CA

"The sex scenes are terrific. I want one of those guys!"
Jerilee – Kansas City MO

"Edgy and sexy with elements of sacred sensuality, although most of the sex is delightfully <u>not</u> so sacred."
Marilyn – New York NY

"Passionate and erotic with shifting realities and time travel. I couldn't put it down. Thank you!
Carol – Shell Beach CA

Isis Erotica

every man's dream

SANDRA GORE

ISBN: 978-0-9853445-6-6

Published by Tajine Publishing, Las Vegas NV

Author website: www.SandraGore.com

Dedicated to Egypt lovers everywhere.

Special
Table of Contents
for the more erotic scenes

The Temple	3
River God	16
The Bath	27
The Wynn	37
The Challenge	86
The Sash	94
The Bite	101
The Boyfriend	127
The Tunnel	149
Night Visit	154
Phoenician Ship	179
Full Circle	197

Table of Contents

The Red Mirror

Chapter 1	The Temple	1
Chapter 2	Obsession	8
Chapter 3	River God	15
Chapter 4	Sit-hathor	19
Chapter 5	The Bath	25
Chapter 6	Encounter	31
Chapter 7	The Wynn	37
Chapter 8	The Nile	44
Chapter 9	Wizard	49
Chapter 10	Temple of Min	52
Chapter 11	The Feast	60

The Persian General

Chapter 12	The Hunt	69
Chapter 13	Lion	77
Chapter 14	Ishtar	84
Chapter 15	The Sash	92
Chapter 16	The Bite	100
Chapter 17	Falcon	106
Chapter 18	Rescue	114
Chapter 19	The Fortune-teller	121

The Great Green

Chapter 20	Hermes Trismegistus	137
Chapter 21	Antinous	149
Chapter 22	The Commander	154
Chapter 23	Escape	161
Chapter 24	The Great Green	169
Chapter 25	Antinous Thrice-Greatest	177
Chapter 26	Cleopatra's Barge	183
Chapter 27	Full Circle	192
Cast of Characters		201

PART ONE

The Red Mirror

Chapter 1 The Temple

It took a few moments for my eyes to adjust to the shadow. Narrow sunbeams, filled with tiny golden flecks of dust, slanted from small openings near the roofline to the polished stone floor. A jewel-colored forest of carved columns surrounded me. The only sound was the soft echo of distant chanting. The air was hot and so very, very still.

I tried to moisten my lips, but no saliva came. I couldn't swallow; I barely could breathe. The pounding in my ears drowned out the chanting, and I heard nothing but the beat of my heart.

At first I thought she coalesced from the clouds of incense. That's how suddenly the young girl appeared. Her small, high breasts were bare, her nipples an unnatural deep red against coppery skin. Bowing her head, never looking into my eyes, she draped olive leaves mixed with cornflowers and lotus petals around my neck before turning to lead me deeper into the temple. The floral scent of the garland softened the acrid tang of burning aromatic wood.

I resisted leaning my head back to take in the vast ceiling plastered with vivid-colored geometric patterns, trying to absorb as much as possible without being obvious. But I couldn't stop my eyes from traveling everywhere at once.

Shimmering hieroglyphs in colors bright as neon exploded from every surface. Soaring murals in vibrant reds, yellows, and blues depicted strange rituals performed by giants with mystical crowns or the heads of animals.

The girl led me to a small chamber fogged with frankincense; hundreds of alabaster lamps glowed. A surge of energy jolted me the moment I passed under the lintel with spread golden wings. Instantly aware of each cell in my body, I vibrated from deep within.

Women as graceful as sea nymphs moved about in long white gowns like my own; the glide of their sandals was silent on the stone. Sheer linen flowed against the lean lines of their thighs and the slim curve of their hips. Their breasts were also bare, their nipples rising to dark peaks. No one else wore a flower garland.

A hush stilled the room when I entered, and every head bowed low toward me.

The priestesses approached me one after another, each with offerings of blue lotus and woven baskets of figs, dates and pomegranates. When I could hold no more, two ancient women with elaborate headdresses murmured an incantation and took everything from my arms. Their eyes were all-knowing.

I stood without moving at all. I never spoke; no one seemed to expect anything from me but to let them freely touch my body. I didn't feel danger, only reverence. Warm fingers loosened the ties of my long gown and within seconds, I stood naked, the folds of sheer linen piled at my ankles.

The Ancient Ones painted symbols on my arms and then my bare thighs with a kind of black ink. My heart drummed so hard I thought they surely could see it pound in my chest. A faint layer of perspiration rose on my skin. My mouth was dry, but not my sacred valley. My nipples tightened and rose to aching peaks.

Paying no attention to the changes in my body, they continued to draw mystic symbols on my naked flesh, murmuring spells under their breath, each hieroglyph with its own incantation.

They replaced my own necklace and garland with a heavy, beaded collar that finished in a counterpoise down my back to hold it in place.

Flowing around me in a calm eddy of snowy-white mist, the roomful of priestesses sang praises, repeating the word *menit* over and over. I knew, without knowing how, that they sang to the collar, summoning its power.

A thousand tiny beads burned into my flesh. I was a furnace of raging heat.

When the chanting stopped, the chamber was silent as a tomb.

The first sound of the finger cymbals was like a distant tinkle of tiny bells. The jingling grew louder but never brassy. Golden rain tickled my ears.

Drifting toward me through a fog of incense, a woman with the yellow-green eyes of a cat carried a headdress with twin ostrich feathers fluttering at each swaying step. Two tall golden horns framed a shiny, gold disk.

The room of priestesses began chanting again as four hands balanced the solar disk headdress on my wig.

Anet-hra-k Hathor!
Auksh satet-v en Amenta
un uat er Isenkhebe Nefrusobek
Anet-hra-k Hathor!

Hail to thee, Hathor!
O daughter of heaven
open a way to Isenkhebe Nefrusobek
Hail to thee, Hathor!

I imagined myself as a figure in one of the vividly painted murals, but how would I walk?

Finally, the Ancient Ones anointed my shoulders, breasts and belly with musk and led me by both hands toward two tall doors covered with gilt.

The doors opened, and I walked through alone.

Watching me from the shadows were two men. I could just make out the whites of their eyes. I felt their heat and smelled their scented sweat.

My oiled naked body gleamed in the low light. There was a heavy new perfume here, a narcotic smoke that blurred my vision and made air rush in my ears. The chamber was electric. My head pounded, and I felt lightheaded and dizzy.

The sanctum shimmered in gold around a white alabaster statue of a seated goddess wearing a solar disk headdress identical to mine. Her right hand resting on her thigh held a large golden ankh. A dozen glowing lamps at the feet of the Goddess cast a soft light that barely flickered.

Without any conscious direction on my part, my hand moved to a silver shaker gleaming in a wooden case on a black marble pedestal. A graceful silver loop held three delicate rods pierced with dozens of small metallic disks. The gleaming silver handle formed into twin heads of Hathor, the cow-eared goddess sitting on the altar throne.

High, chiming notes teased when I lifted the sacred *sistrum* from its ebony box inlaid with ivory. The men stirred when the seductive music broke the silence. It was so still in the chamber, I could hear them inhale and exhale, together as one person.

Every action was as natural to me as breathing. I held the necklace out from my throat toward the statue, shaking the *sistrum* in a slow, even rhythm that grew more and more feverish. When I opened my lips to sing, the words flowed like magic from me without effort.

"O Hathor, O Divine Cow and giver of milk,
O Goddess of Fertility, O Goddess of wine, music and dance,
O Goddess of Love. We adore you.
We ask your blessings for this Son of the Pharaoh, this First Prince of Egypt."

My voice, strong and husky, vibrated in my throat. The crown of my head pulsed. I no longer felt the weight of the headdress. I was light as air.

The two men moved next to me, one on each side. Taking the

sistrum from my hand, the tall one returned it carefully to its case. The shorter man slowly lifted my headdress and laid it at Hathor's feet. The royal insignia of the Crown Prince hung from a thick gold chain around his neck.

I swayed slightly on my feet while they each stroked my body, four hands caressing my breasts, my buttocks, the insides of my loins. The heavy scent of musk filled my shallow breath.

Together they led me to a divan and lay me down on my back. The two started at my feet and began to suck one toe after another, in perfect unison. Then their wet mouths moved to my ankles, licking the small bones there. They trailed up my calves to the inside of my loins, where like preening cats, they lingered with darting tongues.

A well-practiced team, they lifted my feet to rest just next to my buttocks, slightly on the outside. I lay on fur, spread full open, inviting them to enter.

They licked and sucked and nibbled at the tender skin on the backside of my thighs. Tremors moved through me as they edged closer and closer to the moist valley of desire, taking their time, teasing me, enjoying the straining of my hips and my low cries of anticipation when they came near, then moved away. I was overcome with need. My womanhood begged for their mouths.

But just before their tongues found my sacred lotus, they sat back on their heels and chanted in unison.

"*O beauteous one, O great one, O great magician, O splendid lady.*
The Pharaoh reveres you; give that his Son may live!
Behold him, Hathor, flaming one,
His manhood is straight,
The Son of Pharaoh reveres you, O Gold of Gods,
Give of your milk that he live!"

With that they came to me again and each suckled my breasts, their hands kneading like babes at their mother's teats. I lay on the divan, electric shocks rolling through me, moans reverberating in my throat and chest.

The Prince mounted me while his companion licked my nipples and my open lips with his broad tongue; he did not kiss me, though.

A thick penis slid full inside me, stretching my walls, pulling at my wet tissue. The Prince rocked slowly, his chest rising each time his hips moved forward, thrusting deeper, then pulling out almost all the way, sucking me with him, then ramming deep again, never looking into my face, but only at the other man. The pendant Royal Insignia on its heavy chain swung toward me and back—toward me and back. Would he spill his Royal Seed in me?

As if on cue, he rose up and lay his manhood on my stomach just as a flood of white milk spewed. The other quickly bent and lapped it up with his tongue. Then they leaned forward and kissed each other, the Royal One taking back the semen with an open mouth.

They chanted once more.

"His gift has been given,
He defiles not his gift.
Clean is his offering,
It has come from the Prince of Egypt,
He has cleansed what he offers to Her."

It was over.

They knelt before the statue of the goddess Hathor, and the Prince's partner placed a carved, painted chest on the altar. Not looking back, they opened the heavy golden doors and disappeared.

I lay panting and stunned on the low sofa, aching and throbbing. I put my fingers between my legs and rotated on my screaming lotus, dipping into my wetness. I had to have release. I didn't think I could stand.

The doors opened again, and the Ancient Ones, adorned now in simple wigs with twinkling gold chains, entered. Not saying a word, they came straight for me in the dark, one carrying an alabaster bowl, the other a roll of snow-white linen.

With the tender hands of a mother on child, they cleaned me everywhere with jasmine-scented water. They washed the symbols and all trace of fluids away. I relaxed into the soft fur of the divan and let them cool my fire.

What kind of a priestess was I, anyway?

"The Goddess is pleased, Isenkhebe Nefrusobek," they assured me. "The Pharaoh shall be pleased. The spell of Seth the Destroyer on the First Son of Egypt, the son-of-Horus, has been broken. The Golden One has given the Crown Prince back his manhood."

"Not very likely," I muttered under my breath, thinking it best to keep my doubts to myself until I found out more about where and who I was. But there was no mystery about how I got here. It was the Red Mirror.

Chapter 2   Obsession

I had missed it the first time I walked past. It was only on the way back from my wanderings deep in the maze of the antique mall that I noticed the red aura in the shadows. I hesitated—not quite ready to believe my eyes—and stepped into the stall. Leaning against a Chinese screen splashed with yellow chrysanthemums and orange-breasted song birds was an old dusty mirror. A glowing, throbbing old mirror that breathed.

Inhale. Exhale. Inhale. Exhale.

I caught myself breathing in time with the mirror. Every hair follicle on my body came alive. The touch of wool on my skin was painful; having clothes on was painful. I wanted to take everything off.

"Barb, come take a look. Do you see anything...strange?"

"See what? What's there to see?"

"The mirror, Barb, the red mirror."

"Some old Mexican thing." She dismissed it without another look. "Let's have lunch."

We settled at a table covered in a cloth splashed with yellow daisies. Sunshine poured in the paned window, warming my back, shimmering on Barb's wheat-colored hair. Her latest cut was chin-length with long bangs past her eyebrows. She wasn't wearing her contacts today. Hot pink rectangles framed her small, but all-seeing, turquoise blue eyes.

"No sweets for me." She was firm. "I've gained two pounds."

I secretly craved a fresh scone with Devonshire cream and raspberry jam.

Our tea arrived in a blue porcelain pot with green cozy. Barb's china cup flaunted red roses; violets sprinkled mine. Both sets were edged with gold.

"How was your date?" she asked without much interest.

She poured the tea, holding her angular arms close to her sides, never spilling a drop.

I shrugged and wrinkled my nose.

"I don't think I'm going see him again."

"Another one who's not perfect?"

"Be fair, Barb. He was a bore. Everyone in Vegas is trying to sell you something."

"There must be *some* good men around. They can't all be useless."

Tendrils of steam rose in the sunbeams. My mind went back to the mirror. Even surrounded by chattering ladies, I saw the mirror so clearly that it might have been leaning against the window frame right next to my chair.

Inhale. Exhale. Inhale. Exhale. It still breathed.

"How long are you going to wait for Mr. Right to carry you off on his white horse?"

I took a sip of Earl Grey and braced myself. Barb meant well. And she had earned the right to talk to me like this; she listened to my complaints on a daily basis. But when she got that tight little mouth and her blue eyes went steely, I knew I was in for a lecture.

"You hate your job—and you should. Yes, Ed is a jerk," she nagged. "Most bosses are. Stop feeling sorry for yourself. Do something about it. There's more to life than a party."

I sighed. Barb was right about one thing. I did feel a little sorry for myself.

"I should go somewhere…have some adventure…you know… meet some new men."

"Where would you go?"

"Some place exotic…far away…nothing like here."

I didn't buy the mirror that day or even the next, but I dreamed of it every night—such wild, vivid dreams that I woke in a sweat, sheets entangled in my legs and pillows tossed all around. The technicolor images still played in the cinema of my mind when I opened my eyes to the bright sunshine. I still felt the touch on my skin.

Please understand that a love affair with an object isn't unusual for me. But most of the time the attraction is a one-night stand, forgotten as soon as out of sight. Now and then, I'm seized hard and buy right away. My condo is full of treasures that grabbed me and wouldn't let go.

But the old mirror was special. It had become an obsession— hypnotic and irresistible. I couldn't get it out of my mind. Haunting my dreams, plaguing my days, it drew me back like a wild mating call in the jungle.

I gave my boss some feeble excuse to leave work early and sped to the mall. Of course, the mirror hadn't sold. It waited patiently for me, knowing I would come. The red frame pulsed; the glass shimmered. Phantom fingers caressed my shoulders and trailed across my throat. Moist, insistent tongues teased.

I longed to stand naked in front of it, inviting whatever spirits dwelled there to explore my wet. I would spread wide my limbs and invite all who had ever gazed into this mirror to enter into me.

"Hey, ya wanna make an offer? I can call the owner."

The voice belonged to a fresh, freckled face above a tight T-shirt stretched by broad shoulders and even tighter jeans that did little to mask the growing bulge. He managed to maintain eye contact while checking me out from boot to bust.

The minutes ticked away on a Grandfather clock. My feet hurt in my high-heeled boots, and my lower back screamed for a rest. I sank to a green velvet hassock and refused even to look at the mirror.

It was in the hands of the Universe now. If the price was right, then the mirror was right. It was a simple strategy that absolved me from responsibility. Reacting to the moment rather than planning ahead had become somewhat of a life path. I prefer to call it 'going with the flow.'

I leaned forward to peek around a walnut garderobe. The red glow was not only there, it was more luminous. There wasn't a soul around. I crossed my legs and squeezed my thighs, rocking oh-so-imperceptibly back and forth on the hassock. A warm flush spread through my buttocks. My vagina throbbed. My underpants were drenched.

Who was I kidding? I had no choice. No matter the price, the mirror was coming home with me.

The bulky rectangle wouldn't fit in the trunk or through the doors of my little white convertible. I started the engine and held my finger on the release button while the top eased into its hiding place and exposed the leather seats. Together, Freckles and I slid the mirror into the back, bottom on the floorboard and head sticking up like a passenger.

The sun was just setting in a cloudless Vegas sky. I zipped up my leather jacket, jammed a blue M3 cap on my head, and gave Freckles a quick peck on the cheek.

"Do you need any help unloading?" he offered hopefully.

The kid was cute, but younger than I like. A guy his age should be satisfied with a smile from a woman like me.

Buzzing through rush hour traffic, I glanced constantly in the rearview mirror at the other mirror directly behind me, its red frame secured by seat belts, its glass reflecting the fiery clouds of a Vegas sunset.

I congratulated myself. I was in tune with the Universe.

I pushed a couple of iffy yellow lights—okay, maybe one was red—in my hurry to get home. Somewhere along Eastern Avenue between Tropicana and Flamingo, the dirty old thing from the rejects of an estate sale was christened 'The Red Mirror.'

The traffic light turned red. The vibration of the engine reverberated through the leather seat. My fingers slid under the waistband of my pants and down into the wet. Oh, so wet. I breathed out with a deep sigh and leaned my head back, closing my eyes, stroking gently with my middle fingertip.

The roar of a motor pulled me back, and when I looked up, it was at a blue pickup truck with 'Jack the Plumber' painted in yellow letters on the door. Two men leered down. A face out of Deliverance pressed a nose against the passenger window. Jack—it must have been Jack—leaning as far as he could to the right and still stay in the driver's seat, drooled on the inside of the windshield.

Whoa girl! Slow down. What is wrong with you?

I gripped the wheel with two hands, stared straight ahead and willed the light to change. My lane went green, and Jack was stuck waiting for a left turn. I sped ahead, blaming the mirror for my recklessness. Blame the Red Mirror for everything.

I managed to get the mirror out of the car and lug it to the elevator on my own. The doors slid open to reveal an empty shopping cart. More good karma. Glass side up, I heaved it onto the top of the cart, pushed the button for the 3rd floor and rolled the Red Mirror out the elevator down to my blue-tiled entrance with the Laughing Buddha.

Aisha was just inside the door, purring like a well-tuned engine. Ever hopeful and ready, she rubbed up against my heels, circling with back arched and tail lifted high. Her black fur gleamed in the low light from the red shade of the lamp on the bar.

I leaned the mirror against a white wall, poured a glass of Merlot, lit three fat candles on the glass coffee table and dropped my leather pants to the zebra carpet. Aisha tried to jump into my lap when I settled into my grey leather armchair next to the fireplace. But I had other ideas.

"You can start to glow now, Red. You can start to make *me* glow."

Nothing happened. No red glow, no seductive promises, no phantom caress. I felt no warmth; I felt nothing except doubt. *Please don't let this be another fantasy.*

I could hear Barb. *You bought that old mirror because it turned you on?*

Yes, Barb, the mirror first baited me and then enticed me, but when the seduction was complete, it went cold. Having made me an addict, the mirror refused to give me a fix.

Robbed. I felt robbed.

Aisha snuggled into her favorite spot between my legs; her purr vibrated against my groin. I took another sip of Merlot and studied the mirror. Faint traces of blue and white flowers peeked through layers of grime.

That's when I saw the flash. And then another. Gleams of silver peeked out from black residue and sparked in the candlelight.

Aisha tumbled to the carpet when I jumped up to find a clean cotton cloth and grab a bottle of olive oil from the kitchen.

Sixteen silver struts, barely visible, braced the four sides of the lacquered frame. I could just make out a star pattern in each corner.

Settling cross-legged on the white marble floor, I began to massage one of the silver struts slowly and gently with my index finger, applying just the right pressure through the oil-soaked cloth. Aisha purred on my bare thigh.

I barely noticed the first change. Just a bit of light-headedness. The temperature in the room rose, first very warm, before turning hot. An odd woody, smoky scent, heavy and sweet, went straight to my head. I closed my eyes; my thoughts melted like butter in the sun.

Drugged and dreamy, I drifted outside of time in a velvet sea. I was in darkness, not complete, but shadowy. Gone were my familiar things—the black lacquer table, cherry red sofa and the Pink Lady oil painting that covered one wall. I sensed vague shapes moving in the shadows; tongues of fire licked the walls. Aisha no longer vibrated against me.

The green eyes startled me when I turned back to my reflection.

They should have been my eyes, but these were too bold—so bold—and heavily outlined in black. The woman in the mirror stared straight into my soul. I couldn't look away.

She was exotic, foreign-looking, yet her face was familiar, like someone I knew from a dream.

I had no sense of my body; it was simply gone. Was I still sitting Indian-style on the cool tiles of my living room floor? I felt nothing through my thin panties, nothing at all.

"Who are you?" I whispered. The words swam to my ears as through deep water.

There was no response. I tried again.

"Can you...see me?"

Apparently sound couldn't cross the glass because she gave no sign of having heard. Instead, her hand came up and adjusted a stray lock of jet black hair. She lifted her chin and angled her head slightly, looking straight at me with those emerald green eyes.

It was in the way she tilted her face, and the satisfaction in her look, that gave it away. She wasn't studying me at all, but admiring her own reflection. I saw her, but she didn't see me—a strategic advantage.

I touched myself. Yes, everything was there. I had come this far without harm. The Universe opened a door to something magical— an adventure. I had only to step through the Red Mirror.

Chapter 3 River God

I never understood how it happened, but the chorus of a thousand songbirds shattered the silence, and I opened my eyes to another world. The air was rich with the sweet perfume of flowers and the earthy scent of loam. The bare whisper of a breeze kissed my skin.

I reclined in a long gown of white linen pleats on a plush carpet of green grass in a protected garden lush with palms and flowering trees. Birds sang from every branch. Brown sparrows, yellow finches, blue warblers—I had never seen so many birds. Hundreds of nests peeked out from the ornate capitals of stone columns.

Not far away, at the end of the grassy lawn, flowed a wide river where the last traces of mist melted in the rising sun. Distant brown cliffs on the far bank brightened to gold. The sky was azure blue without a cloud.

I stretched out my legs and wiggled my toes. My muscles were well-toned, my thighs firm. I felt deliciously fit. I must walk a lot. I liked the new me.

My fingernails and toenails were stained rust-red. Tiny geometric designs trailed across the tops of narrow feet, and a crisscross pattern encircled my ankles. At first I thought the designs were tattoos before I realized they were painted and recognized henna from photos in an old National Geographic.

From the look of my soft hands and pampered alabaster skin, I led a privileged life. A ring with golden horns around a grape-sized lapis lazuli stone gleamed from the middle finger of my right hand.

Two heavy gold bands coiled around thin upper arms. They felt like they had always been there, molded to my flesh. A wide gold collar around the base of my throat fastened with a short length of chain falling down my back, under my hair.

Only it wasn't my hair. It was a wig. My head itched under the shoulder-length mass. I pulled the wig off; the fresh breeze caressed my bare scalp. I dared to scratch, ever so gently, not hard at all, still a little timid to touch this new body. I ran my fingertips around a wide mouth with full lips and then felt a familiar cleft in my chin. My neck seemed as long as a swan's.

I was me, but not me, all at the same time. I wasn't at all afraid, though. In fact, I felt more relaxed than I could ever remember.

My pubic hair was gone; a mound the same dark rose color as my nipples showed through the linen. No underwear at all. Did everyone walk around like this?

I breathed slowly, drinking in the perfumed air, savoring the kiss of breeze on my skin, exploring the impossible slim curves of my belly and thighs. I lingered on my breasts while my nipples rose in the sheer cloth that concealed nothing. Yes, I do believe I like this new me.

"Isis!"

I had a name, the name of a goddess. I also had a man. At least I saw one coming right at me—a River God of bronzed flesh and snowy linen.

A stiff white kilt wrapped around his hips and ended just above the knees. He wore nothing above the waist except a wide, beaded collar. A blue and white striped triangular headdress framed his face. His broad shoulders tapered in a triangle to a narrow waist.

The bare skin of his chest glowed like burnished stone. His thighs and calves were taut, the elongated muscles of a runner. I wondered if he also was without underwear.

When I took his hand, and he pulled me to my feet, his exotic scent went straight to my head. I reached out to run my fingers over his bronzed chest, down his flat belly and under the snowy kilt.

I was never this bold on the other side of the mirror. I wanted to touch him, to fondle him, to make him quake with desire.

He grew instantly hard as an iron post, but instead of encouraging me, he took hold of my hand teasing his manhood and raised it to his perfect lips. I touched his moist tongue. His eyes never left mine. He teased me with a half-smile full of promises.

We stood very close, almost nothing between us. I smelled the myrrh in his hot scent. His mouth, both hard and sensuous at the same time, had been chiseled by a master sculptor in a softer stone. I willed the perfection of those lips to explore every inch of my body. Could he not feel the waves of my desire crashing on his shore?

The thick, black *kohl* lines around his dark eyes were drawn almost to the temple. He had an angular face with cheekbones that might have been too sharp in another man, but not River God. There was nothing about him that didn't sear me. I felt his heat right down to my bones.

My fingertips as light as the wings of a butterfly stroked the smooth muscle of his chest. Slowly I traced down his biceps and along his forearms to the wide gold bracelets at his wrists. The tiny hairs on his skin rose at my touch. He leaned close, his full lips at my ear, his breath hot and moist on my neck.

"Not now, Isis. Not here."

He stroked once across the hollow of my throat; I felt the wet on the inside of my thigh. Would he touch me there?

"I shall come to you later and drink of your nectar," he breathed in my ear. "You shall fly to the stars with my tongue on your lotus."

Then he stepped back, his arms at his sides. He had the erect, rigid posture of a military man.

"Come. You will be late for the Temple."

Temple? Bile came up in my throat. I looked carefully at River

God. If he saw anything different about Isis, he didn't show it. His seductive half-smile held no hint of suspicion.

We walked side by side, not touching, down a stone path just wide enough for two. It ran perfectly straight through a garden aflame with color and shaded by date palms, sycamores and rows of almond and fig. Fountains gurgled like natural springs into vast rectangular pools covered with green lotus pads. Tall white blooms trembled on slender stalks.

The tiny bells in my wig tinkled at every step. The sheer pleats of my gown hugged my thighs. Graceful and light on my feet, I felt perfectly in tune with my body. I could be a dancer.

River God kept silent until we reached a wide avenue with a phalanx of stone sphinxes marching down each side. A sea of foot traffic flowed in both directions, but no one hurried. Many eyes turned toward me. A group of men in long white skirts bowed their shaved heads as they passed.

"Your Nubian slave awaits you," River God said.

A Goliath with oiled ebony skin stood as erect as a statue. His biceps were like ripe melons; his thick thighs bulged. Striated scars from some age-old Nubian ceremony covered his cheeks. His onyx eyes were careful not to look directly at me.

"I shall come in the heat of the afternoon," River God whispered as we parted. "When the others are sleeping."

Others? My throat closed. I felt dizzy and slightly sick at my stomach. Heat rose off the pavement in shimmering waves. The sun overhead was white-hot. I watched River God move through the bronze bodies in snowy linen until his blue-and-white striped headdress disappeared in the crowd.

That's when I followed my slave Goliath to the temple with the goddess Hathor on the throne in the inner sanctum. That's when I was meant to cleanse the Crown Prince and cure him of Seth the Destroyer's curse. That's when I failed. That's when my troubles began.

Chapter 4 Sit-hathor

It hadn't taken me long to recover from the shock of my ritual with the First Prince of Egypt and his scribe. I cared nothing about the Crown Prince's manhood or the Pharaoh's ambitions. I had done my job as high priestess. What happened in the Temple, stayed in the Temple.

Fussing with my body, muttering incantations, the Ancient Ones never ceased praising the healing power of the Goddess as manifested through me. But they hadn't been in the inner sanctum to witness the sharing.

When they finished cleansing me of fluids and soothing me with warm oils, I hurried through the incense-filled ritual chamber and past the forest of columns to look for Goliath.

I was thinking only of River God's promise of a flight to the stars, when a short fat priest with a large amethyst dangling from his earlobe stepped from nowhere into my path. A soft leopard skin draped his fleshy shoulder. There was something odd about him that I couldn't quite place; I sensed no sexual energy at all.

"Isenkhebe Nefrusobek," the priest squeaked. "Sit-hathor, The Highest-of-High, Golden of the Golden One, High Priestess of the Two Lands awaits Isenkhebe's presence in her private audience hall."

He addressed me by my formal name in the high pitch of a

eunuch. It was clear that Isis had no patience with him. I stifled an impulse to laugh at his voice and lowered my lashes so he couldn't see the derision in my eyes.

Soft echoes of chanting resonated along a stone corridor lit by tall torches in deep alcoves. We finally reached tall, double cedar doors mounted with golden lionheads. The priest put his hands on the heads and leaned with all his weight.

Suddenly, the doors swung wide open into the blazing light of a thousand brass lamps. The wild chorus of high-pitched male voices stopped in mid-note when I entered. The chamber was so still, I could hear the lanterns consume oil.

The eunuch priest then stepped to the side and inclined his head toward me.

"Enter," his silence commanded me. *"Sit-hathor awaits you."*

His swinging amethyst earring splintered the light.

I had heard him clearly, yet no words passed his lips. He spoke directly to my mind. Could he also read my thoughts? If he had suspicions about my presence in Isis, he gave no sign. His black eyes were as fathomless as a deep well in the desert.

He backed out of the chamber, closing the doors as he exited, leaving me with a roomful of staring men.

"Isenkhebe Nefrusobek, my child, come nearer that we may look upon you and feast on your beauty."

The voice of liquid gold belonged to a striking woman in her middle age seated on a dais covered with a carpet of richly-dyed wool. The four legs of her chair were carved limbs of a lion ending in massive claws at the feet; the chair arms were capped by gilded lionheads.

She might have had an iron spine, she sat so straight against the low back. Her forearms rested on her thighs, like the statue of Hathor in the temple, but she held nothing in her hand, no golden ankh, that I could see.

"Come closer," she repeated, holding out her right hand to me.

I sank to my knees, brushing my lips to the ring on her middle finger, a giant lapis lazuli set in gold horns, identical to mine.

"It has been too long, my daughter. Our duties are many; the hours are few. We have reports of your superior talents. You have trained well. You bring us great pride."

Her lips curved into a small smile without showing any teeth. Heavy black lines framed her eyes; blue mica sparkled from her lids, up to her eyebrows and out to her temples. A wig of thick waves, shimmering in a golden mesh, reached to just below her chin.

She placed her hand on my bowed head, and I instantly felt her energy like the buzz of a swarm of bees. An intense current flowed from her into me, spreading quickly from the crown of my head right through to my womb. My cells ignited. I felt on fire.

"I have a mission for you, Isis," she whispered only for our ears. "The time is full, the need great, and you are ready."

Mission? My head jerked in surprise, but her hand kept me from pulling back. I felt the pressure of each fingertip, even through the wig. Her energy flowed stronger. My brain liquefied. All thought disappeared. I was overcome by the lust to mate, like a cat in heat.

Then Sit-hathor took her hand away and the current stopped as abruptly as a plug yanked from a socket. But every nerve in my body still burned. I still throbbed.

"You are the flesh of my body and a piece of my *Ka*," she crooned. "You shall not neglect to serve your Goddess."

"My mother, my mistress," I murmured. "It is said that the work of the Goddess Hathor is what acts upon women. I pray that the task you set before me is in alignment with Her path for me."

I'd never seen anyone change so quickly. Her lush lips shrunk to a hard line. Her shiny black eyes, huge just seconds before, nearly disappeared behind narrow slits. I thought she might strike me down with a look.

"Would you doubt the will of Hathor, Queen of Gods? She has spoken as clearly to me as I now speak to you."

The ice in her voice chilled me even in the sweltering heat of the closed room. The hum in the chamber around me grew to a roar. This was not going well. When I next spoke, I was careful to please.

"My mistress, giver of my life, the fault in every kind of character comes from not listening. My ears are full open to receive your words. My heart is full open to fulfill your wishes."

Sit-hathor morphed again; she warmed instantly, smiling ever so slightly, but still not showing her teeth. The tension in the room eased with a collective sigh.

Leaning forward, her face just inches from mine, she pressed a gold charm into my hand. Tiny glyphs saying "one-who-has-entered-the-heart" formed a single large glyph for "heart."

"By this amulet, your father will recognize you as his daughter."

I must have looked shocked at her words, because she put her long fingers under my chin, drawing me even closer to her face.

"Yes, you have a father," she hissed. Her black eyes flashed a warning that she would brook no opposition. "The time has come for you to meet him."

She settled back in her chair and breathed out a long sigh. With her breath flowed a seductive energy that swirled around her, slowly spreading outward, drawing everyone in the chamber to her as a queen does the hive.

"Prepare for a river voyage, my daughter. Put your trust in the eunuch Qeb-ha."

No! Not that fat little freak with only half his manhood. I envisioned his pathetic little manhood, dangling limp and alone, with no plump scrotum for me to fondle and suckle.

"Allow the whisperings of the Goddess to enter your heart." Sit-hathor's tone had softened somewhat; she was almost kind. "Even a fool acts wisely if he follows his heart."

"There is no protector save the Gods," I intoned.

Then she signalled that I should rise; the interview was over. But before I stepped away, her inky eyes, huge in her pale face, held mine for a long moment.

"Know well, Isenkhebe Nefrusobek, that there is nothing left but the doing."

I had forgotten that it was day. The sun was a white disk in the washed-out sky when I left the dark temple through the courtyard with columns crowned by carved heads of Hathor with cow ears. I blinked and shielded my eyes from the harsh light. The fat old priest Qeb-ha came out of the shadows and stepped again into my path.

"Do not resist," he said clearly. Only his lips didn't move. *"You are the chosen one. It is the will of the Goddess."*

He startled me, coming from nowhere again and speaking with no words. I shuddered in spite of the stifling heat and tried to take a deep breath to calm myself, but there was not enough air in the open courtyard for me to breathe.

"We sail at dawn," he said in his repugnant squeaky voice, but at least he spoke out loud.

Tomorrow I sailed with the castrated old priest who could read my thoughts. Who knows how deep he could probe?

I brushed past him in a panic to get away, to get to River God. I had to make the most of my time before dawn.

I would caress River God's smooth, unquestionably male body, stroking down his chest and across his belly to settle on his undamaged manhood. I would knead like bread his cherished nuggets and watch his throbbing organ swell with desire.

Goliath the Magnificent waited where I had left him under the lintel adorned with green-and-orange outstretched wings. My eyes traveled from the white triangle of his headdress to the white triangle of his loincloth, noting his massive chest and rippled abs along the way.

I moistened my lips and dreamed of the dark places I could taste. I pictured my tongue sliding up and down the giant's swollen rod, nibbling the glistening tip with my sharp teeth. I would scratch his balls with my long nails while I sucked him dry. But not too dry.

Yes, I would command the Nubian to service me if River God

had come and gone. Goliath would do just fine.

Chapter 5 The Bath

Chaos greeted me at the small villa set in a lavish garden behind
white walls. I could hear the high voices, all talking at once, before
I came in the door. More than a dozen chests, large and small, were
scattered on the mosaic floors. A bird-like woman surrounded by an
electric field screeched orders at everyone. Egyptians were not always
calm, after all. She stopped only to tell me that Maia was packing
my jewels and potions.

There seemed no chance now for a stolen afternoon with River
God. Even Goliath was out of the question, certainly not here and
now.

When I entered my bedchamber, a delicate young girl prostrated
herself, kneeling with her forehead to the tiles, her palms on the
floor, fragile arms stretching on the bright-colored mosaic of wild
geese flying above marsh grass. Silver bands fastened scores of plaits
in her glossy black wig. She held herself so perfectly still, I wondered
if she breathed.

"Rise up," I said. Then I whispered in the hushed tone of a
conspirator, "Did he come?"

She blushed and lowered her eyes.

"Yes, Isenkhebe Nefrusobek, he came after the second meal."

Maia avoided looking at me. Thick lines of *kohl* extended out toward her temples, and mica sparkled on her eyelids. A muscle in the corner of her mouth twitched, and for a moment, I thought she might cry.

"He did not speak to me, Mistress. He entered this sacred chamber through the forbidden door, but left when he saw the preparations for our holy journey."

My guess was that River God would be back. He wouldn't let me leave without a visit to my bed. His touch in the garden told me that. The packing couldn't go on forever. I still had tonight.

I would always do my duty to the Goddess, but I had my own needs, and they would come first. The plans of a god are one thing; the thoughts of men are another.

I settled on a mound of pillows and sent for roast duck and unwatered wine. Maia brought me a black purring cat.

"Will Pehtes travel with us?" she asked.

"Oh course. Who else shall I caress on the long nights?"

Pehtes settled in my lap, between my thighs, just like Aisha.

"Is that not right, Pehtes? I fear you will be stroked on this voyage more often than me."

The Sun God Ra disappeared behind the golden cliffs across the Nile. The nightly battle in the Underground with *Apep* the serpent had begun. As always, it would end with a victorious Ra rising as the new dawn.

Curtains of the finest linen embroidered with blue and gold ankhs billowed around the low bed. The scent of gardenia and jasmine drifted on the warm evening breeze.

Maia lighted alabaster lamps with scented oil and floated white lotus blossoms in preparation for my evening cleansing. A heavenly cloud of rose-colored sheer linen canopied the portico around a pink marble pool. Small colored-glass bottles of perfumed oils stood at the water's edge. A nightingale, the only sound in the new night, sang just outside.

Sinking into liquid velvet the same temperature as my body and the evening air, I closed my eyes. I had waited for this all day. I was one with the night and the bath.

He was silent; I sensed his presence rather than heard him. My first sight was bare feet and sturdy ankles not a yard away. My eyes travelled up straight runner's legs to feast on an engorged penis standing straight up, head glistening in the lamplight.

O Hathor! You are indeed the Highest-of-High.

River God was in the water before I could move, straddling me, pushing me back into the unyielding stone of the pool wall. I didn't complain.

I kept trying to get my head down, to taste him, but he teased me and traced his hard penis along the bridge of my nose, brushing around my lips, over my chin, down my neck and then rubbing back and forth across my nipples. He held my hands and wouldn't let me touch him. I was maddened by the need to draw his erect manhood deep into my throat.

He eased into the water on top of me, his hardness pushing against the softness of my belly. The back of my neck pressed on the unforgiving edge of the pool. I stretched my tongue to lick at his swollen knob, but his mouth was at my ear.

"Isis, do not move, or my seed will issue. I want it to last."

Releasing my hands, he pulled me full into the pool; I floated on my back, white lotus blossoms with dazzling yellow centers swirling in eddies around me. My nipples rose from the water; the aureoles of my breasts were dark circles just at the surface. On his knees beside me, his erection pierced the clear water.

He started with my closed eyes, then my eager mouth, his lips not touching me, but blowing warm puffs of air like a gentle wind across my skin. His breath was sweet with a trace of myrrh. He blew softly in my ear, down the side of my neck, and across the base of my throat.

I floated on a cloud of divine pleasure; the water was warm on my back and the air warm on my face, shoulders, and breasts. His breath, warmer still, moved to my nipples. He blew round and round each taut tip, never touching, but lingering until they rose so tight and tall that they stood like miniature obelisks.

His hand slid between my thighs. I opened wider, but that was all. I was content to do nothing, to exert nothing, to have no will of my own. His finger came from underneath and stroked my swollen bud in small circular movements, with almost no pressure. I drifted in a timeless dream.

Strong hands encircling my ankles, he pulled my knees past his ears, draping my legs over his shoulders. I still floated among the sweet-scented blooms. His hands cupped my buttocks while he lowered his head and raised me to his lips. His tongue swirled my throbbing lotus.

He sucked, and then played with his tongue, and then sucked again. When the roll of spasms swept through my womb, the walls of my vagina contracting over and over, a long, vibrating cry escaped my throat into the deep silence around us.

River God's mouth was on mine in an instant.

"Sh-h-h, Isis. The household is awake and nearby."

Too late for that. By now, every eye in my household looked to my rooms. Every ear strained to hear more.

He stood up in the pool with the water reaching mid-thigh. His body had gone tense and his erection slack. I could feel every taut nerve in his body. River God knew he tasted forbidden fruit.

My hands in his, he drew me slowly to my feet. We stood inches apart, water streaming off our skin aglow in the hazy light of the alabaster lamps. The air was sweet with perfumed oil.

The sound of my heart pounded in my ears as my breasts rose and fell with each breath, in and out, in and out. I wanted nothing other than to feel him inside me—filling me, sucking me—the way the prince had stretched me in the inner sanctum.

"They will stay away," I assured him in a throaty promise. "I have given orders to be alone."

He hesitated. Slowly the corners of his mouth turned upward in his secret half-smile, and he was mine again.

His lips were full and dry and covered mine with ease. His tongue slipped into my open mouth, exploring slowly, never hurrying, always taking his time, relishing every touch. He sucked gently on my tongue and drew me to him with his muscled arms. My breasts crushed into his broad chest; his nipples were hard points. I arched my back, pressing my pelvis into his. His erection was back and between my clenched thighs.

I found myself outside of the pool, with no memory of exiting. We glided backward, two bodies moving as one, as he led us to the bed with billowing sails. The curtains brushed our bare flesh but didn't cling; our skin had dried in the desert night air.

We sank together onto the cushions of a bed designed more for pleasure than sleep. Smelling the mating scent, Pehtes purred round my ears.

I lay spread on soft linen, my shaved head resting among cool silk pillows and warm cat fur. River God's mouth was on mine again in a deep lingering kiss probing with his tongue. His touch was more sensual than sexual. He savored me as one does a fine wine, something precious you loathe to finish.

I had a sudden thought.

"Sail with me tomorrow. With you in my bed by night, I can face anything by day."

Startled, River God stopped his caress and stared at me in shock.

"I cannot do that. I am as bound to my duty as you are to yours."

His voice was incredulous. I might have asked him to fly.

"You could appeal to the Governor," I insisted, even though alarms rang in my head. "I am the daughter of Sit-hathor. I am in need of protection. Who better to protect me than you?"

He changed in that moment. I felt him begin to pull away. When he spoke, his tone was already distant with a note of patience that one uses with a child.

"Isis, sweet and dangerous Isis, you know that our destinies were foretold when we came from the womb."

Time slowed. I could almost see the thoughts turning in his head. The nightingale sang sweetly, unaware that the world had changed. The air, now utterly still, was abuzz with the hum of insects. The cries of night creatures carried from the Nile.

I panicked as I felt him slip away. Reaching out, I traced my fingers lightly along his forearm. The hairs rose, and I took hope.

"I feel alone. I do not want to go on this voyage alone. I fear it. I fear everything about it."

I pleaded with him, but in my heart, I knew he wouldn't go with me. This journey was for me only—and Qeb-ha. It was as Sit-hathor had said. *All that is left is the doing.*

He stroked my face, then along the bone at the base of my throat out to my shoulder. I was like a cat before him. Pehtes tried to crawl into my armpit; I wanted to follow her there.

"I desire you more than any woman I have ever known or seen, Isis." His voice was gentle and low, barely above a whisper. "But I must place myself away from you. The Gods have set us on separate paths. Mine is to serve the Pharaoh, yours the Goddess."

He paused to watch his fingers trace the mound of my breast. How could he touch me while saying goodbye?

"The great glory of a wise man is to control himself in his manner of life."

I hated those words. I wanted to put my hands over my ears to keep them from entering. It was my fault. I was too needy. I had gone too far.

He bent and kissed my lips with lingering tenderness. A chisel split my heart in two as cleanly as a piece of granite. The pain pierced my soul.

"The fate and fortune that come, Isis, it is the Gods that send them."

I had been taught a thousand ways to make a man desire me. Now there was nothing I could say or do to make him stay. He was gone as quickly and silently as he had come. I had a terrible feeling that I would never see him again.

Chapter 6 *Encounter*

The bells kept ringing and ringing, louder and louder. Would they never stop?

I felt Pehtes purring against me, but when I looked, it wasn't Pehtes. It was Aisha.

I was back. The cold marble tiles of my living room were hard, and my back hurt. How long had I been lying there? Had it been hours—or days?

What was that incessant ringing? It stopped, and then started again. I found my cell—I *really* had to change my ringtone—on the coffee table next to my keys and checked the caller ID before answering. It was Barb.

"Where have you been?" she demanded. "Didn't you get my messages?"

"Barb, I have to tell you something."

"Tell me when you get here. I'm at the Stirling Club."

"But, Barb, listen—just listen. I bought the Red Mirror today."

"What red mirror?"

"The one I showed you. The day we had lunch."

I heard live music in the background. Then Barb said to someone, "...a glass of Chardonnay, please."

"It has some kind of...power, Barb."

"Power? What are you talking about?"

"That's what I wanted to tell you. I sort of got...well...turned on...looking at it." My plan was to lead up to River God, but Barb wasn't focused at all.

"Looking at what?" she snapped.

"The Red Mirror, Barb, the Red Mirror."

"You got turned on by a mirror?" Then she whispered, "Have you been smoking something?"

"I had this kind of...dream. Only it wasn't a dream. At least...I don't think it was. I was myself...but not myself...and...and I was in Egypt. You know...when there were Pharaohs...and stuff like that."

It sounded ridiculous, even to me, when I said it out loud.

"Forget the pharaohs," Barb snorted. "I'm here with two gorgeous men. They're buying drinks and making intelligent conversation. I repeat, *intelligent* conversation. You can tell me about this Egypt dream later."

"But Barb—"

"Here's your choice," she interrupted. Her voice took on the sharp bossy tone that signals she's run out of patience. "You can stay home with your mirror and go on some kind of fantasy trip. Or you can put on your stilettos and get over here where a real-life man is waiting for you."

"But—"

"And *please* don't tell me you have to think about this."

"Okay. Okay. I'll be there in half an hour."

"You're not going to regret this. Who knows? He might be Mr. Right."

The cell phone went dead. Barb had won. I hadn't put up much of a fight.

I saw Barb at the bar at the same time she saw me. Tall and thin like a model with platinum hair, she's easy to spot in a crowd. She smiled and waved discreetly. Perched on one of the high, leather bar chairs, she faced two men standing with their backs to me. One was blond, the other dark-haired. I already liked the square of their shoulders and the cut of their suits. Money and confidence. I could see it from across the room.

"Hi, Barb! I made it." I kissed her on the cheek before turning around.

My knees went weak, and I gasped out loud. Barb grabbed my arm and kept me on my feet. Standing just in front of me, dressed in a charcoal silk suit with a blue paisley tie, was River God.

Well, River God with green eyes. Green instead of dark; green like mine. I had the sense to realize I was staring at him with a gaping mouth and snapped my teeth together. If he recognized me, he didn't show it, but had the same amused half-smile on his face as the morning I first saw him on the banks of the Nile.

Tailored to fit perfectly over his broad shoulders, his suit narrowed at the waist. It took no effort at all to visualize the triangular torso underneath. He looked straight at me, or I would have glanced down at his muscular thighs to picture the generous, good parts between.

His sensuous lips had been carved by the same master sculptor. He had thick black hair now, styled in an expensive salon cut. He was shorter. No, he was the same. I was wearing three-inch heels, and my eyes were on level with his luscious mouth. I stared at him. The other three stared at me.

"You look exactly like someone I used to know," I said lamely. I couldn't think of anything else.

His half-smile was amused, but inviting. He might not recognize me, but he was definitely interested.

"You look like you could use a drink." His voice was incredibly, impossibly, the same.

In fact, everything about him was the same as River God, except his suit and hair—and the green eyes. Barb introduced him as Rasheed. His blond Nordic friend was Lars.

We settled in one of the small rooms just off the lounge, semi-private, with walls covered in traditional oil paintings in gilt frames. An ochre velvet sofa was against the wall. Plush velvet armchairs, one on each end, formed a U around a low, gleaming mahogany table.

I sank into the down-filled sofa cushions and crossed my black-silky legs. My skirt rode up to mid-thigh. The red patent of my heels shone in the yellow light. Rasheed eased into the chair at the end of the coffee table, just to my left.

He radiated an energy that was both animal and sensual. Just sitting next to him rendered me helpless and without a will of my own. I sensed that he knew it. But he kept cool with that slightly amused, seductive smile curving his lips.

Rasheed didn't try to make conversation, but looked around, observing. I decided to be silent and mystical—like Isis. I glanced slyly at the muscles of his thighs stretching his silk trousers and barely resisted spreading my legs, opening myself to his touch, inviting his fingers to my wet.

Sipping my Plymouth martini, toying with the olive on a plastic stick, I studied him from under lowered lashes. It was not my imagination. Rasheed looked exactly like River God. But more than that, he *felt* like him. It was the way he moved and his voice—and the way his eyes, even though clear now, instead of dark and mysterious, probed for secrets.

I thought he'd forgotten me. Then he suddenly turned and caught me staring at him. The corners of his lips curved up again ever so slightly, and he leaned into me, the silk fabric of his suit tightening across his shoulders. He didn't try to hide the bulge in his pants. I could smell his cologne, faint but exotic.

His look was magnetic. I couldn't have torn my eyes away if I wanted to.

"I know," he breathed, tracing his middle finger lightly over my knee and up a few inches toward the hem of my skirt. "I really feel you, too."

An electric shock ran straight up the inside of my thigh.

"Listen to me. Don't say a word." His voice was low and urgent. "I want you to come with me to my hotel. I don't want you to say no."

I felt a twinge of fear. He looked and sounded like River God; he even *felt* like River God, but could I trust Rasheed to *be* like him?

Intense heat radiated from his body; I burned as if next to a furnace. The power of his muscles pulsed in his silk suit.

He put his hand on my upper thigh, very close to the Gateway to Pleasure, searing through layers of fabric and stocking. I envisioned a brand on my flesh in the shape of his palm.

"You don't have to worry about anything happening that you don't want," he said.

I looked at his mouth only inches from mine and knew there was only one thing I wanted.

When he leaned forward and brushed my lips with his, he was tender. He put his fingers in my hair and kissed me again. His tongue found mine. He was gentle and full of longing.

"I desire you more than any woman I have ever known or seen."

His words riveted me; they were word-for-word the same as 2500 years ago—or was it only five hours? I couldn't make sense out of this; it made no sense. But he had said those exact words to me before, and then walked away. I wasn't going to let that happen again.

"Okay," I whispered and nodded my head. "Okay."

Standing in the hall by the lounge entrance were two men, both over six feet, well built and well-dressed in tailored suits. They fell in behind us, following closely down the wide staircase and out the leaded glass doors.

A valet came up immediately. Rasheed nodded, and the taller of the two men handed the valet the claim ticket. My internal warning light flashed red. I hadn't agreed to go anywhere with three men.

Rasheed leaned close, touching my elbow. I felt his breath in my ear.

"Marcos and Gamel go everywhere I go. They are always close to me. There is no danger. But I need to keep it that way."

Go everywhere he goes? Are we talking about *bodyguards*?

"I have my own car." I felt a tiny bit panicked. My voice was edgy, the pitch a little too high.

"Gamel will bring your car." Rasheed was calm, his voice reasonable.

The shorter man looked at me briefly and then away. His hair was shiny black. His silk suit stretched across the bulk of his shoulders. I imagined I saw the outline of a gun at his armpit.

Rasheed's assuring eyes, almost olive in the marquee lights, told me, *This is going to be fine. You are safe with me.*

I saw only River God and opened my bag and handed him the stub. A limo pulled up and the other man—did Rasheed call him Marcos?—climbed behind the wheel.

Chapter 7 The Wynn

Rasheed had a suite at the Wynn, in the tower with private entrance and check-in. We rode the elevator in silence to the top floor. Ceiling-to-floor windows looked out on Trump Tower and the blazing lights of Vegas Valley. I was aware of nothing but the heat of Rasheed's body. When he put his hand on the small of my back, my flesh blistered. Quiet words were exchanged with Gamel and Marcos, and they disappeared.

"They will stay away. I've given orders to be alone," he breathed in my ear as his arms went around my waist, pulling me back into him.

Hadn't I said the same words to him in my pink marble pool with white lotus blossoms?

He lifted my hair with one hand and held me tight with the other. He kissed each vertebrae down the back of my neck and between my shoulder blades. How did our bodies just melt into each other?

I still had on my heels; my pelvis tilted into his. I felt him grow hard as stone against my hips while his hand moved from my waist down across my belly. He pushed hard on the tip of my womb with the base of his palm, his hand cupping my mound, burning hot through the knit of my dress.

I moaned low in my throat. I wanted him to stroke me like a cat.

I would roll onto my back and give him my belly, my legs spread wide.

His hand traveled down my loin to the knee and then up the back of my thigh to caress my buttocks, all the while kissing the nape of my neck and my shoulders. He let my hair fall. His free hand found my breast. When he touched my erect nipple through my bra and my dress, I cried out.

We stood like that for an eternity, my back to his front, his hands stroking me all over. We swayed back and forth, something primordial coursing through our veins.

Then he turned me in his arms and kissed me long and deep. I pressed my thighs against his and felt him huge on my belly, an iron post. When I put my hand down to fondle him through his trousers, it was his time to moan.

Low lights burned in the room; a mirror covered an entire wall, reflecting our silhouettes against the Vegas night sky. I glimpsed a lush king bed through an open double doorway.

He eased the zipper of my dress, the slider inching slowly past each tooth. I unbuckled his belt and unzipped his pants. He slid my dress off my shoulders and it dropped to my ankles, bundling on top of the shiny red heels. I slipped his trousers down his thighs, and they fell to his polished loafers.

We didn't say a word. We didn't even kiss. We wanted no distraction from the unveiling.

I helped him out of his jacket, loosening his tie and lifting it over his head. His starched shirt was snowy white in the red and black room. I undid every tiny button and slowly unfastened the gold cuff links at his wrists. When the shirt came off, I had my first sight of his bronzed chest and flat belly. No doubt about it, this was River God. I licked his erect nipples just once.

My fingers tugged at the elastic band of his trunks and pulled them down. I labored to breathe. Heart pounding and blood rushing all around inside my head, I went to my knees and took him in my mouth. He filled me almost to the throat. My head slid back and forth, pumping. His body shook, every muscle tense and rock hard.

"Do not move," he whispered with his hands on my face, lifting me to my feet. "I want it to last."

More words from the past. Was this real or a dream?

His hands slid around me, undid my bra and eased the straps off my shoulders. He was slow, deliberate, not in a hurry. My breasts were swollen white mounds with blushing halos, nipples aflame. He took one in each hand and a sound caught in his throat. His face took on a new light.

He moved his thumbs back and forth, back and forth, across the inflamed tips. I arched my back to bring my hard, aching nipples closer to his lips, begging him silently to take me into his mouth. At the first touch of his moist tongue, I would explode.

Instead he slid one hand under my panties and between my thighs. He brought back his hand, looked at his dripping fingers, and spread my own wet on my breast.

The first rolling wave of an orgasm washed through my womb. I moaned louder with each surge. If he had not held me fast, I could not have stood.

Without hurry, he eased my panties down past the slim garters to join my crumpled dress. Panting, near sobbing, I lowered my head to his chest. I didn't know a body so limp could still stand. He held me stable, dragging my clothes away with his foot as I shifted balance from one leg to the other.

At last, I stood naked in black silk stockings, black and red garters and red patent shoes.

He kicked his own clothes away and faced me, swollen knob glistening, erection probing the air. His hands were on my hips, pulling me forward, sliding his rod between my clasped legs. I locked my thigh muscles and rocked back and forth, astride him, riding at a slow pace. His hardness was pressing on my swollen bud throbbing again with life.

Engorged beast between my clenched legs, he walked me backward to the bed, moving us as one person. Like dancers in a waltz, our eyes locked in a spinning room, he lowered me, his eyes fixed on mine.

He kissed my forehead, then each eyelid, the tip of my nose and then full on the mouth, his lips smothering mine, sucking languidly, his tongue penetrating and unhurried. Lingering long over each kiss, he still took his time.

I was wild to feel him inside me, to fill me, to pound me. But I surrendered on the lush covers of the bed and let him do with me what he willed. He knew every sensitive spot to touch and exactly how much pressure to bear. He knew my secret places and laid claim to them all.

His finger hooked under the elastic of my left garter and slipped it slowly down the long length of my leg and over my foot. He rolled the stocking carefully over my knee, along my calf, and past my toes. One kiss on the arch of my foot, and just as slowly, he removed the right garter and then the stocking, ending with his lips on each toe. He kissed the shallow red marks left by each garter, first high on the left thigh, then on the right.

When I first felt his tongue on my clitoris, I actually relaxed—home again after lifetimes of being lost.

He sucked and licked and sucked more. His teeth teased while shocks jolted my body. An electric current pulsed through the soft under-bottom of my buttocks. When he sensed my need unbearable, he pulled himself up the length of my body, and I felt the tip of him at my gate. I wrapped my arms around his broad back and thrust my hips toward him, begging him to plunge deep.

And then, at last, he was full inside me. We both exhaled deep at the same moment, a long sigh echoing across eternity. At first he didn't move. We breathed in and out together. My vagina pulsed, on fire, swallowing him whole.

Like a starved beast, he began to devour me. He pounded and pounded, his hands grasping my buttocks to give him more leverage and better control the rhythm. I raised my legs high into the air so that he could plough deeper still.

Lust replaced tenderness. Animal sounds growled from our throats. A wave crested and a rapid succession of endless contractions of pure ecstasy rolled through me. His body convulsed, froze, and then shuddered. He collapsed on top of me. I could feel his heart throbbing in his chest next to mine.

We slept. I slept. The sky was barely light when he woke me. Rasheed was dressed in a fresh shirt, pressed suit, and a blue tie. His eyes were shiny bright, glittery like emeralds. I looked up at him in surprise.

He sat on the bed next to me and traced my features with his fingertip as if he were memorizing each one.

"I have to go now."

"But—" I started to interrupt him.

He placed his finger on my lips.

"Sh-h-h-h. Listen to me. There are things I can't tell you. Things you mustn't know. It's better this way."

I stared at him in disbelief. He wanted secrets after last night? We'd been like one body, no division, nothing separating us.

"When will I see you again? I don't know anything about you. I don't have your cell number—or your email." I was in a panic. For a microsecond I even thought of Facebook.

"I know how to find you." He smiled his secret half-smile, not of amusement, but sweet with longing.

He could walk away though; he had the strength for that. He leaned down and kissed me with such tenderness my heart cracked, again with the same chisel. The pain this time was also the same.

"We have known each other before, Isis, and we will know each other again."

"No-o-o-o!" I cried out.

But he was gone.

Barb called just as I got home to a hungry cat. I put food in Aisha's bowl and turned on the kettle while Barb shouted in my ear.

"Why haven't you called me? I've been worried sick!"

She paused, but not long enough for me to answer.

"Are you okay? TALK to me!"

"Everything's fine."

"You don't sound fine. What the bloody hell happened last night? I can't believe you went off with that Rasheed guy."

She paused again and then asked a little fearfully, "He didn't hurt you, did he?"

Did breaking my heart count? But I knew what Barb meant.

"No, he didn't. . .hurt me. He wouldn't do that."

"How do you know? *Mr. Mystery Man with his bodyguards.* He scares me. I'm sorry I got you mixed up with him."

"I'm not."

Silence.

"Are you home?" Then she whispered, "Are you with *him?*"

"He's gone, Barb. Gone."

"Unlikely," she snorted. "Lars told me Rasheed's Coptic. That's some kind of Middle-Easterner; you know how obsessive they can get."

"Trust me. He's not obsessed. He walked right out the door. And don't be sorry about last night. Calling me was exactly the right thing to do. I'm not sure you had any. . .choice. I'm not sure any of us had any choice."

"Choice? What are you talking about?"

Then she remembered our phone conversation before the Stirling Club.

"You never told me about the mirror. What was that Egypt stuff about?"

"I'll have to tell you later, Barb. I need to go."

There was no way I could go to work. I called in sick, turned my cell off and sat at my laptop, sipping Assam tea with milk from an old X-Files mug. Aisha crawled into my lap.

'Copt-Wikipedia' came up in the Google search. I skimmed the religious part explaining that Copts are modern day Egyptian

Christians, and then read, "Copts are direct descendants of the Ancient Egyptians."

I looked over at the Red Mirror. I had no idea how any of this was possible, but I was not crazy—or dreaming. I never felt more sober or awake in my life.

Next I googled 'Hathor.' A photo of the goddess in the temple popped up. If it wasn't the same statue, it was close enough. I tried to remember if I'd seen it before, to explain how it appeared in my dream. But I didn't really believe I had dreamed about Egypt. Rasheed had called me "Isis." I heard him clearly. There was no doubt in my mind, at all. Rasheed was River God, and he knew it, too.

Vegas bookies wouldn't give odds on the chances of our meeting at the Stirling Club. The Universe put us together for a reason, and I wasn't leaving our path to fate or the gods. I had the Red Mirror. I was going back.

I curled up in my gray leather chair with Aisha and stared at the mirror, replaying each sight and smell, each change in the room. How did it begin? The cleaning! The transition started with the cleaning, or rather the rubbing. Rubbing was the key. The comparison to Aladdin's lamp was obvious; this was some genie I had summoned.

I put out extra food for Aisha and filled her box and a plastic dishpan with clean litter. I made sure the lid was up on the toilets, if she needed more water. The bottle of oil and the cloth were still beside the mirror.

Metal strips gleamed all around the frame. I rejected trying another strut; I needed to return exactly where I had left. I'm not much of a scientist, but remembered from chemistry class that you have to limit your variables.

Sitting cross-legged on the floor, just like yesterday, except dressed now in sweats, I picked up the cloth. Aisha snuggled against one thigh. She was already familiar with this routine. She liked it; she knew it meant I would stay put for a while. At least, that's how it would seem to her.

Chapter 8 The Nile

It was utterly still except for a hum in my ears. I drifted with no birdsong, no sound of hammer on stone, no rustle of the wind through the palms. The hum was not constant, but more a repeating subtle rise and crest, a kind of "swoosh," somewhat like the sea trapped in a conch, but without any hint of a roar.

Golden sunshine filtered through saffron drapes. Not even a faint breath of breeze relieved the heaviness in the air. A light layer of perspiration swelled on my skin.

I sat straight up. Not in my gardens, not in my chambers, not at the Temple, I wasn't anywhere I recognized. The river! The swooshing sound was the current of the Nile as it swirled under and all around me. I had come back, but after we sailed from Thebes. How would I find River God now?

I could easily see through the sheer drapes onto the deck and beyond. Below me lay a dozen or more men sleeping under awnings hung for shelter from the fire of the sun. The banks of the Nile were distant bands of green against tall dunes bleached white in the glare.

The boat was long and narrow. My pavilion divided the barge in two with just room for a man to pass on the sides. Both the bow and stern of the ship were carved into bundled papyrus reeds. Long wooden oars with blades at the ends leaned against the low sides.

Only the steersman at the massive pole-like rudder was awake. A blue-and-green winged cobra covered a square sail, lifeless now in the afternoon doldrums.

Bodies stirred in the corner nearby me. Young women lay on mats, very close to each other. I counted four from my household, plus me, all in this small cabin filled with chests. The journey was going to be even longer than I feared.

"Does Isenkhebe Nefrusobek require my attention?"

The old priest Qeb-ha stood just outside with only the filmy weave of the drapes separating us. The last thing I wanted was the attention of an old, useless eunuch—useless at least to me.

Behind him, I saw Goliath rising from the afternoon sleep, his skin glistening like polished ebony in the sunlight. The muscles across his shoulders rippled as he adjusted his white kilt and headdress. His legs were twice as long as Qeb-ha's and powerful enough to break the eunuch's neck with one squeeze.

The pleasure from my River God was great beyond compare, but yesterday's drunkenness does not quench today's thirst. I needed satisfaction, and I would have it with Goliath.

"Qeb-ha." I tore my eyes away from the Nubian. "When we moor for the night, I wish to bathe in the Nile. The day has been long and hot."

Qeb-ha stepped quickly forward to the curtain.

"Isenkhebe Nefrusobek is aware that the God Seth waits in the shadows for the innocent to lose their way."

"I shall take the Nubian for protection. He looks as if he could battle Seth Himself and emerge the victor. Please arrange it."

"As Isenkhebe Nefrusobek desires," he muttered out loud. His silent words were louder. "*It is in women that good fortune and bad fortune are upon the earth.*"

The afternoon faded into long shadows. I nibbled dates and pomegranates and drank watered sweet wine. Pehtes purred in my lap while I played endless games of *senet* with my ladies, throwing sticks and moving pieces around the safe and danger squares. The Sun god Ra was low on the horizon when we pulled into the port of Abydos.

The city lay at the end of a canal from the Nile; I hadn't expected such a crowd at the riverfront. Boats of every size moored at the long stone quay. Sweaty dockers swarmed the wharfs like a colony of ants. Small fishing canoes made of bundles of papyrus cruised up and down the river, hawking tilapia and perch from the Nile. Qeb-ha was busy dickering over price. He needed several baskets of today's catch to feed the crew.

Everywhere I looked I saw clusters of merchants trading mountains of Egyptian grain for ivory tusks from Sudan or earthen jars filled with oils and wine from Cyprus. I saw no place I could hide in the rushes with the Nubian.

I had daydreamed all afternoon of the cool of the Nile on my skin, of rising from the water, my body wet, my nipples erect. I would order Goliath to follow me into the grasses and lie on his back. I would lick him and suck him until he was a stone post. He dare not touch me; he would be too afraid.

And then straddling him, slowly—so slowly—I would lower myself onto his giant pedestal. I could never sink all the way. My throbbing lotus would scream out each time I moved up and down his shaft. I would dangle my ripe breasts in front of his thick lips, teasing him with a forbidden fruit he must never taste. And when my aching bud fully flowered in its lust, I would throw back my head and call out to the Goddess as tsunami waves crashed in my surf.

Oh, it would have been divine. But even I could see it was not possible this night, in this place.

The moon had just risen. Qeb-ha came to the edge of my pavilion on the boat. The reed curtains were lowered; I was reading a papyrus scroll by the low light of an oil lamp. We had just returned from a bathhouse near the docks, not the bath of my daydreams, but the perfumed water had soothed my frayed nerves and calmed my fire.

"May I enter, Isenkhebe Nefrusobek?" Qeb-ha's high-pitched voice pierced my resting ears.

What could I do? I nodded to my ladies, and they disappeared into the night.

"Isenkhebe is reading. May I inquire what?"

"I am studying the course of the river to Saïs and the cities along the way."

"Yes, most wise. Sit-hathor would be pleased to see that Isenkhebe is using her time well."

"Better than at the river with a Nubian?"

If he was shocked, he didn't show it.

"I am certain Isenkhebe's mother would advise her to enjoy herself with whom she wishes, as long as no fool joins her."

"Would that be me, or he who joins me, who would be the fool? Or would being with a fool, make one of me also?"

He was not the only one who could talk in riddles, but he didn't rise to the bait and only shrugged his stooped shoulders, folding his hands neatly in his lap.

The air was much milder now, pleasantly warm. My skin was cool and dry. A soft caftan folded along the curves of my body. The silver tassels in my short wig matched the thin bracelets around my ankles. I wondered if I could find a hidden corner of our narrow ship to pleasure myself with Goliath.

"What does my father know of me, Qeb-ha?"

"He knows Isenkhebe is well-schooled in languages and math. It is he who has chosen the tutors."

"And of my life in the Temple?"

"The Gods choose our paths when we come from the womb."

Those were River God's words when he left me in Thebes. How would I find him again? The map told me that we had sailed one, maybe two days to the north.

Small waves lapped against the hull and the stone quays. Night birds called out and were answered. I could hear the oarsmen playing *senet.* They gambled as usual, their voices animated and loud. The decks of other ships were also alive with raucous laughter and shouting; heat-weary crewman and tradesmen relaxed in the cool of the night. Their voices carried easily over the water and through the breathless mist. My handmaidens were not far away; their laughter was a medley of tiny bells.

"We must play *senet*, Qeb-ha; I would enjoy a meeting of minds on that battleground."

"It is in battle that a man finds a brother—or sister. It is on the road that a man finds a companion. It is my wish for both."

He seemed perfectly at ease with me. I was certain he couldn't see deeper than the Isis who sat before him. His face was placid and plump and remarkably unlined for his age. Did the absence of male hormones make him more youthful in the way it made his voice falsetto? The fat of his belly lay in rolls. His breasts were as generous as some women.

Why wasn't Goliath with his glossy taut skin stretched over bulging muscles sitting next to me instead of this puffy old man?

"I am who I am, not by my own choosing," he said as solemnly as possible in his high-pitched voice. "Man, even a godly man, cannot alter the life the Gods assign him."

My face went hot; he had read my thoughts. I busied myself with a sip of wine, avoiding his eyes. Isis was a prejudiced bitch at times. Qeb-ha had not chosen to be castrated any more than I had chosen to service the powerful in Hathor's Temple.

"We sail in the morning for Khent-min. May the Goddess protect Isenkhebe and bring sweet dreams."

And then he rose, bowed low, and moved clumsily through the break in the reed curtains. I was left alone with my own ideas about sweet dreams.

Chapter 9 Wizard

The wind blew hot against my scorched skin. Sweat evaporated into the dry, brittle air before it could form beads. My parched throat burned; I was blinded by the glare of a golden disk filling the silver sky.

A cobra slithered into my path and raised his hooded head to glare into my eyes. His back curved in an S; his tail coiled upward. His forked tongue flicked my cheek. Clear drops of venom oozed from the spiky tips of two fangs. I tried to scream, but as wide as I opened my mouth, no sound came. It was a silent world.

With wings spread wide, a vulture swooped down, seized the cobra in razor-sharp talons, and carried him off in a cloud of red dust that blocked the sun.

When the swirling dust settled, a white-haired man in a blue gown with shining stars stood a stone's throw away. He raised a silver sword above his head; the rays of the sun exploded off the tip in a bright burst of white light. In his other arm, he cradled a rectangular green slab, engraved with words I couldn't read, no matter how hard I tried. I knew that I should follow him, but when I took my first steps, he was there and then he was not. I was alone again in a vast empty space. I was alone in the Universe.

The earth cracked; a massive gash yawned and green water rushed forth. A lake began to rise and rise, filling the whole desert until it reached my knees, then my thighs, and then my waist.

I struggled to wake up, but couldn't. I was trapped. Was I to drown in the High Desert? Could someone drown in a dream?

My mouth moved; my lips formed the prayer, *Hathor, my mistress, Gold-of-the-Gods, do not desert me!* But no sound came. It was still a silent world.

A falcon landed on my shoulder, and Hathor spoke in my ear. "How do you expect to understand what is going on up in the sky, if you do not even see what is at your feet?"

I looked down; a hippo swam by my legs. I grabbed hold of her ears with both hands and pulled my body onto her back. The hippo turned her massive head with immense liquid eyes and whispered, "I am Hathor, my beloved Isis. Why do you not trust me to carry you to your fate?"

"Isenkhebe Nefrusobek! Come back to us!"

The only water was under the boat. There was no hippo, only the frightened face of Maia on her knees beside my bed. She was in her sleeping gown. Her head was bare, and her scalp glowed in the light of the clay lamp she held in her hand. There were no lines of *kohl* around her eyes. She was frightfully pale. The others, sitting up on their mats in the corner, stared at me with round eyes.

"My mistress was in the Land of Dreams. I feared she would not return. I called and called, but Isenkhebe Nefrusobek was too far away to heed my cries."

"May I enter?" Qeb-ha asked anxiously from outside the curtains.

I nodded numbly to Maia, who opened the slit in the reeds. Qeb-ha rushed to my side. He took my wrist and placed his fingers on the pulse. My heart was pounding like a gazelle hunted by Berber dogs. Qeb-ha looked carefully into my eyes, seeming to reassure himself that I had returned. His concern was so great, I wondered if some never came back from the Land of Dreams. I felt like I almost didn't.

"Hathor was with me in the desert—" I started to explain.

"Do not speak of it. Words could summon the dream world to the real world."

"The Goddess was trying to tell me something, Qeb-ha, but her words were just riddles."

"The dream could be a warning. The Gods created the dream to show the dreamer his blindness. A blind man will stumble on any path, even well-paved. How can he hope to navigate a road fraught with danger?"

Now that I was fully awake, the dream fragmented into vague bits of memory, pieces of a puzzle I hurried to assemble before they disappeared.

I called for papyrus and ink and began frantically writing down the images, struggling to recall the right sequence, but the details slipped away faster than I could write. I felt desperate to record the dream before it was lost. I saw cobras and vultures but could attach no meaning to them. I recognized Hathor in both the falcon and the hippo, but who was the Wizard? What was written on the green slab?

No one spoke. They watched me as I wrote. They seemed frightened by my intensity. I don't think they were convinced I had fully returned. Or perhaps I had come back a different person.

Qeb-ha didn't leave until I finished. Maia brought me a cup of watered wine. I drank with great thirst in huge gulps, and lay back exhausted. I felt cold, then hot, then cold again. Pehtes pushed her wet nose on my cheek and kissed me with her dry scratchy tongue. If I had been away in the Land of Dreams, she didn't know it. How simple life must be to a cat. How simple life used to be for me.

Chapter 10 Temple of Min

Screaming baboons in a nearby sycamore grove awakened us before daybreak. Wood smoke blended with the thick morning mist; the sleeping jetty came alive with workers hurrying to make the most of the day before the heat rose. Our crew finished the rest of last night's broiled fish; they drank beer and ate beans with cone-shaped loaves of bread before casting off for Khent-min.

The winged-cobra sail unfurled. Our barge entered the current of the Nile and was swept downstream. Marshy reeds and high dunes lay on the west bank. The low desert came right down to the east bank of the river and spread in a flat expanse of sand to the distant hills. Oars rising and falling, the rowers sang a rhyme that kept them in beat as the shore moved swiftly past.

After massaging perfumed oil into my skin until it glowed, my ladies lined my eyes with *kohl* and dyed my lips and nipples deep red with pomegranate juice. The slim cut of my sheer gown molded to my breasts, hips and belly. Nothing was left to the imagination. I chose a shoulder-length wig doused with gardenia essence and plaited with yellow silk tassels.

With Goliath leading the way through the busy streets of Khent-min, I went straight to the Temple of Min, the god of male fertility.

It was easy to find. A wide, crowded street lined with billboard-sized paintings of Min with his sacred erection led straight to the pylon.

Just outside the pylon gate, I stopped at a stone vendor's booth.

"Would the priestess care to trade a blessing for a fine statue of the God Min?"

The vendor gave me lewd smile showing black teeth. His hungry eyes didn't hide his lust. They traveled from my nipples to my ankles and up again before meeting my eyes.

"Give me that small basalt statue," I teased him, "and I shall bless you with a faience crocodile charm to make your Min rise. Let us pray that one charm is enough to aid such a needy member."

He laughed. Even more black teeth showed.

The Min statue fit neatly in my palm. I stroked the smooth, glossy stone with my index finger. Jet black and naked, the city's patron god held a flail in his right hand and an erect penis in his left. All Goliath, my own black god of fertility, needed was the whip. Would I use it on him or command him to use it on me? Which would bring the greater thrill?

"The priestess has her own Min, I see," remarked the vendor with a smirk. He nodded his head in the direction of Goliath.

"If the Nubian is the lady's taste, she can find more like him at the Temple."

The Temple was eerily quiet after the din of the city—and dark. Long shafts of dust-filled sunbeams angled to a polished stone floor. Vast murals covered the walls. Most depicted the giant-phallused Min seated at a banquet table piled high with *cos* lettuce oozing white milk from its tall leaves. White bulls and barbed arrows covered a forest of square columns.

The inner sanctum of a Hathor temple is forbidden to all but the initiated. No outsider would ever be allowed. But if the handful of Min priests busying themselves with offerings objected to my presence, they didn't show it.

A nine-foot statue carved of black basalt with a phallus as long as a man's arm and as thick as a log towered over the chamber. Kneeling at the stone altar, I placed a garland of lotus blossoms at Min's massive feet and sang a hymn of praise.

Min, Bull of the Great Phallus
You are the Great Male, the owner of all females.
The Bull who is united with those of the sweet love,
of beautiful face and of painted eyes,
The goddesses are glad, seeing your perfection.

The room was hot and the air thick with frankincense, but not thick enough to mask the smell of sex. Two priests in a trance ejaculated into silver bowls like the dozens already at Min's feet. The worship of Min must take many enticing forms, the best hidden in secret sanctuaries behind closed golden doors.

I wandered down a narrow corridor, lit by torches in niches shared with basalt Mins with his erect member. Goliath followed close behind. If I didn't stumble on an obliging priest, then I would find a private corner and measure the Nubian's bounteous manhood against the new standards set by these black statues.

We turned a sharp corner, and the hallway dead-ended in a closed wooden door decorated with brass studs. I heard lyre and pipe music on the other side, and the sound of chanting. These voices were deep, not at all like the high-pitched chorus in Sit-hathor's temple.

I quietly lifted the latch and eased the heavy door open a crack.

A dozen men or more, all nude, engaged in the worship of the almighty phallus. One bent over, sucking the engorged penis of one man, while another penetrated him from behind. Another penetrated the second man until they formed a complicated endless knot of copulating men, who at the same time performed *fellatio*. Even I, trained in a thousand ways to give pleasure, had never seen anything like this.

A low dais dominated the end of the small chamber; two men lay back in low chairs. I recognized them at once as the Crown Prince and his scribe who had shared me in the temple.

The Prince, his face in a trance, was being serviced by two pubescent boys busy at his crotch. A great wreath of lotus blossoms draped his nude chest. The Scribe lounged in a chair of carved phalluses with a young child not more than ten between his legs.

Their depravity had certainly not been cured by our ritual in Hathor's Inner Sanctum. With the boy's hair gripped in his fists, the Scribe jerked the child's head back and forth, back and forth, in a wild, ruthless rhythm.

Maybe it was my thought of the Goddess that disturbed his psyche. I'm certain I didn't make a sound. But the Scribe suddenly looked straight at me. His eyes widened, and he sat up, pushing the boy's head away. His evil rushed at me like a thousand buzzing hornets.

I shoved the door shut with my shoulder, leaning into it for just a moment to stop shaking. My heart hammered; my palms sweat. I turned to Goliath to motion for us to get out, but it was not the Nubian who stood behind me. The metallic insignia of the Royal Guard flashed in the torchlight.

A hand went over my mouth; another grabbed my upper arm, dragging me around the corner and pushing me through an open doorway. There were no windows and no lighted lamps. It was black as the darkest night. The flicker of torches cast dancing shadows in the hallway outside.

I struggled to free my arm, but the weight of the soldier's body crushed me to the wall. Sobbing from terror, I tried to bite the hand on my mouth.

"Say nothing, Isis," he whispered. "Nothing at all."

O Hathor, I worship at Your feet for the gift You have brought me!

The voice in my ear was River God. My whole body trembled so violently, I'm not sure I could have stood if he hadn't held me up against the wall. Instead of sobbing from terror, I burst into tears of relief.

"Listen to me—and listen to me carefully. These are dangerous men—capable of any evil. You must leave now—no hesitation—now! This is no time for your foolishness."

"But I thought you were in Thebes," I whispered. His touch felt real enough. His scent was real enough. But I still feared I was dreaming.

"The Pharaoh commands me to escort the Crown Prince to Saïs."

I heard the words but was only aware of his heat. I kissed the base of his throat, above his leather chest armor. He tasted of sweat and myrrh. In spite of the tension, I felt him harden against my womb. Our bodies were so taut that one flick of a finger would shatter us into a million small pieces. I was as fragile as glass.

I put my hands on the back of his head and lifted my face to his. He resisted for a brief moment, and then gave in. The hardness in his mouth softened; he was as tender as the night of the bath, as tender as the night at the Wynn.

My life force flowed into him; I was hardly aware of where he ended, and I began. Our need for each other bound us so tight, we might have been shackled in chains. But he had the strength to break away.

"Now go. Go! You were never here. Do you understand? You were never here."

He released me from the wall, took my arm more gently, and steered me down a new corridor, the Nubian on our heels. I heard voices in the distance calling out, "Guard!"

Bright sunlight blinded me when he pulled open a small red door in the rough stone wall. It was a tiny side street, not more than four feet wide.

"Do not speak of what you have seen to anyone, Isis. Do you hear me—anyone?"

He didn't follow us into the alley but closed the door without a word of goodbye.

O Hathor! River God and I traveled the same river. We both sailed to Saïs. The Universe wanted us together. My feet didn't touch the pavement all the way to the boat.

Qeb-ha had returned to the barge and was frantic with worry. I didn't even try to hide my thoughts from him. I was both terrified and euphoric. I understood nothing, except two equal and powerful forces had shown their faces to me in the Temple of Min.

The evil of the Scribe had enveloped him like a black cloud of pestilence. I saw it in his eyes, even in the dark. But my River God loved me. O Hathor! He loved me. I could still smell his desire and need on my skin. His taste lingered on my lips, honey sweet.

"I think we should set sail, Qeb-ha. I do believe the Gods would approve."

To my surprise, Qeb-ha didn't reprimand me with a lecture on the dangers of Seth in the night. He stood very still; I could feel him probe my mind. I didn't try to block him.

He studied the banners of the royal barge moored but a few hundred yards away.

"Yes, the moon is full, the river broad," he said at last. "There can be greater dangers than the peril of Seth the Destroyer. I shall ask the Gods to forgive our arrogance that we sail tonight."

Maia lowered the reed curtains, closing out the sights of Khent-min. My heart told me to get away—and get away fast.

Time on the river stood still. Lone fishermen balanced in their shallow papyrus canoes and cast their nets onto the glassy Nile. We flowed past verdant fields more like clusters of gardens than farms. Laborers toiled naked in the hot sun, repairing the irrigation canals after the yearly Inundation.

I kept looking behind us, expecting at any moment to see a sail emblazoned with the Shield and Crossed Arrows of the Saïte Dynasty, but there was no sign of the royal barge. Having rowed through last night, we would stop for this one.

Ra sank below the cliffs on the far bank. The sound of animals hunting and being hunted carried across the dark water. Great crocodiles with hooded eyes lay in waiting, their long, thick, perfectly still bodies camouflaged in the mud.

A herd of hippos upstream growled and thrashed about; they could turn ugly and lethal in an instant. An angry bull could crush a fisherman's bones between his massive jaws with one snap. Our men would sleep on the boat.

The cook prepared the evening meal on clay, charcoal-burning stoves. The crew ate their regular diet of broiled perch, onions and beer. My ladies and I dined on salted oxen leg and cold roasted duck with cucumbers and goat cheese, dates, and watered wine. Of course, everyone ate bread, always bread.

Qeb-ha ate quietly by himself and didn't join the idle conversation. His face was lined with worry.

"What do you fear, Qeb-ha?" I asked. "What do you see?"

"I see Isenkhebe is no stranger to trouble."

"But surely you can read my heart and see that it is pure."

"One cannot know the heart of a woman any more than one can know the sky," he grumbled.

"Do you truly fear what I might do? What of your pledge to be companions on the road and brother and sister in battle?"

"Isenkhebe is a reckless woman of little patience. That gives me much to fear."

The whites of his eyes gleamed in the starlight; his amethyst was only a tiny glint in the shadows.

"Can I not convince you, Qeb-ha, that my faults lie only in small things?"

"Small things are also worthy of respect, Isenkhebe. The little bee brings honey. The little locust destroys the grapevine."

"It is a wonder I was chosen by the Goddess, if so unfit."

Qeb-ha for once had no response. The grunts of restless hippos rumbled not far away. The crew slept, exhausted after so many hours of rowing.

Millions of jewel-colored stars twinkled in the vast inky sky. The desert was black, no lights anywhere, on either side of the river.

Meskhetiu, the Ox Foreleg constellation, pointed to the unchanging Star of the North.

The god Horus had torn off the leg of the evil Seth and hurled it into the heavens to guide travelers through Seth's land of chaos, the Desert.

Chapter 11 The Feast

Four colossal stone baboons greeted us at the waterfront of Hermopolis, city of Thoth, God of the Moon and Healing. We docked south of the Eastside commercial district at a yacht harbor for luxury barges. Hermopolis was known for great learning, but also great wealth.

Qeb-ha came to me with an invitation to a banquet on the Westside where merchant princes competed to build the most splendid palace. My ladies emptied the clothing chests to find exactly the right gown. The exquisite gossamer linen clung to my body like film. My skin, oiled and perfumed, glowed like fine ivory. My mound, my nipples and my lips were stained the same deep red.

In honor of Thoth, I chose an amethyst and garnet necklace with dangling gold baboon charms. Hathor, bare-breasted and surrounded by graceful nude dancers, adorned my hinged armbands. The lapis lazuli ring, identical to Sit-hathor's, dazzled from my right hand.

More gemstones strung on gold threads twinkled in the glossy waves of a black wig. Turquoise stones decorated sandals too fragile for walking. Maia painted ground mica and malachite on my lids up to my brows and outlined my eyes with thick lines of *kohl*. Accented by jet black bangs, my eyes glittered a startling green.

She drenched my body and wig in oil of gardenia. We held nothing back. Even those who saw me every day turned to stare.

Muscular Nubians, poles lifted to their massive shoulders, carried us in one-person litters hung with silver bells and red tassels. The townspeople stopped and bowed low as we passed along wide avenues lined with shade trees and lavish white mansions painted with murals of hunting scenes.

A naked servant girl with cobra tattoos round her nipples greeted us with garlands of cornflowers and led us to the head table flanked by low chairs with yellow linen cushions embroidered with blue ankhs.

Hundreds of small lanterns cast a flattering light, but not bright enough to dim the night sky. Nightingales in gold cages sang out to each other. A double row of lotiform pillars surrounded the fountain courtyard; the waning moon had just risen.

There was just enough breeze to scatter the petals of myrtle trees planted in glazed ceramic pots. Purple snow flurries drifted to polished stone and floated on small rectangular pools.

Qeb-ha was well-respected in this house. Our host Ankh-hor embraced him warmly and seated him at his right side and then insisted that I should sit on his left.

Ankh-hor, a high nobleman in favor with the Pharaoh, had a wide, ready smile that showed two missing teeth. His gold armbands looked too heavy for him to raise his chalice to drink. A broad pectoral of lapis lazuli and turquoise beads woven together with filaments of gold covered his mahogany chest.

An army of servants carried trays laden with ostrich and duck eggs, cucumbers and *cos* lettuce. We nibbled on Cyprus olives and mounds of fresh goat cheese while watching young girls bend and twist to the music of finger cymbals, harps and wooden pipes.

Delicate gold chains hung round the dancers' slender hips; gold serpents encircled their upper arms. Dyed the deepest of reds, their nipples popped against alabaster skin. Tiny silver bells in their elaborate wigs tinkled as seductively as a *sistrum* in Hathor's Temple of Love.

Servants entered again with giant silver platters of baked swans stuffed with quails and pigeons that had been dressed in turn with dates, almonds and cracked wheat. Whole fattened cranes, simmered in goose fat and sycamore figs, arrived next.

But the highlight of the evening was roasted game, seasoned with rosemary or cumin and garlic. Only the hunt could put ibex, gazelle and aardvark on the table.

I praised our host Ankh-hor for his generosity and exquisite taste.

"I cannot get my fill of the wild game, Ankh-hor. I relish the savage taste of the beast who has fed in the desert. The very air with its raw, heavy scent is captured in the meat."

"Then you shall hunt tomorrow, my priestess. It is my gift to you."

"Is that not exciting, Qeb-ha? I am invited to a hunt! May I tempt you to join us?"

I felt beautiful and powerful, not the woman Qeb-ha criticized. I had drunk too much wine, but in truth, I was more intoxicated by my own charms than by the grape.

Qeb-ha glared at me and squeaked something about "duties."

"Come, Qeb-ha my dear friend, do not be such an old man!" Ankh-hor put his arm around Qeb-ha's shoulder as one would when teasing a brother. "A beautiful woman deserves to be spoiled. I shall send my son. The only thing he loves more than a beautiful woman is the hunt."

Qeb-ha might be able to read my mind, but I can sometimes also read his. He waited for me to decline the invitation, but I didn't. And I was delighted to see that Ankh-hor would not take 'no' for an answer.

"You cannot refuse me, old friend. Would you deny me the promise of a thousandfold return on my gift at a feast?"

A guest could no more deny the wishes of his host than a host could say no to a guest. Qeb-ha's eyes pierced me like barbed arrows.

I refused to look at him. He tried to speak to my mind, but I pushed his silent words from my head.

I was sick of the boat. I was sick of the river. I had not had a man in days. I could at least have a day of hunt. And who knew what could happen in the desert with a hunting party of men?

I saw myself riding in a fast chariot, bouncing over the shining stones under a cloudless sky, hooves thundering on the hard ground with the power of the horses vibrating along the shaft, rising up through my loins to thrill me.

Qeb-ha, cold and fuming, didn't speak all the way back to the barge. My ladies were undressing me when he slipped inside the curtains without asking permission to enter.

"Do not go on this hunt, Isenkhebe Nefrusobek."

"But I have accepted the invitation, Qeb-ha. What excuse could I give?"

"Say you are ill. Say anything, but do not go." In his fury, he addressed me directly, as an equal.

"It is you, Qeb-ha, who constantly remind me of my irresponsible behavior. Am I now to change my mind on a whim, and then lie?"

"What of our mission?"

"There is small risk in one hunt, Qeb-ha. I do not ask that we delay our voyage."

"A high-priestess should not hunt; a high-priestess should not kill. How dare you take this risk, when there is so much at stake? You disgrace your mother with your selfishness and arrogance!"

I had never seen Qeb-ha angry. His voice was impossibly high-pitched. My ladies stood to the side with their eyes cast down. No one moved. I don't think anyone breathed.

I deserved this hunt and a day of freedom. Still, Qeb-ha's disapproval weighed heavy on me. He saw things no one else saw.

"The Nubian will be at my side," I argued. "Ankh-hor's son will lead the way. There is nothing to fear. The Goddess has chosen me. You said so yourself. She will protect me."

Qeb-ha clenched and unclenched his fists. Would he strike me? As improbable as it seemed, I had a small doubt. He turned abruptly and pushed through the curtains. The flames in the lamps flickered as his stubby body stormed past.

I knew he was right. I don't know why I wouldn't admit it.

As much wine as I'd consumed, I couldn't fall asleep. Maybe it was excitement over the hunt, maybe it was anxiety over Qeb-ha's objections. He had sensed the peril of Khent-min without a word spoken.

Khent-min. I throbbed at the memory of River God's lips, the pressure of his manhood against my belly, his chest on my breasts.

I rose quietly and padded softly across the deck. My ladies slept in the corner; no one stirred. I slipped without a sound through the bamboo curtains into the night. The yacht harbor was quiet. Even the gamblers had gone silent.

The moon had set. It took a few moments for my eyes to adjust to the starlight. The crew lay forward on the deck, wrapped in linen sheets, some curled on their sides, others lying on their backs like mummies. Goliath should have been easy to spot among the Egyptians; his mass was double that of most. How delightful to feel at last his 'double' manhood probe my womb.

But the Nubian was not to be seen. I looked all around the open deck. Mosquitoes buzzed round my ears. One bit me on the forearm and I squashed it. A tiny spot of blood showed on my skin.

"Does Isenkhebe Nefrusobek require something?"

Qeb-ha startled me. Curse of Seth, I hated his squeaky voice.

"Where is the Nubian?" I asked boldly.

Goliath was my slave. Could I not do with him as I pleased?

"He is with Ankh-hor's men preparing for the hunt."

Even in the starlight I could see Qeb-ha's small smile at my disappointment.

"Is there something I can do?" he asked.

I glared at him. He knew what I wanted and that a eunuch was useless.

Swirling my swollen lotus with my fingertip dipped first in my wet canal, waiting for sleep that wouldn't come, I pleasured myself with images of a muscled Nubian or bronzed Egyptian pounding me against the rail of the chariot.

All the while, sniffing the mating scent, tossing their silver-twined manes, massive stallions snorted and pawed the ground.

Anything could happen. Something would happen. I would make sure it did.

Tomorrow was the Hunt.

PART TWO

The Persian General

Chapter 12 The Hunt

The small lodge made of mud bricks with a palm thatch roof stood on the East Bank at the top of the first rise from the Nile. A thick grove of sycamore trees provided shade. Chariots with restless horses stirred up golden dust; the brass trim of carts and gold-studded vests glittered in the bright rays of Ra rising.

Built for speed, the chariots were so light that a single man could lift one easily onto a boat. Imported birch and elm formed the frames, wheels, and axles. The carts had leather fronts, decorated with paintings of date palm branches or two rearing horses facing each other. Only the wealthiest could dream of owning a hunting chariot.

Packs of long-legged Berber hunting dogs ran in circles, tongues hanging out. They snapped and growled at each other, but didn't fight.

Groups of men in short white kilts and leather vests drank beer and ate barley bread; Ra flashed off the tips of their spears. Their laughter loud and raucous, they no doubt exchanged tales of their conquests. I recognized some from Ankh-hor's feast last night across the river in Hermopolis. They saw me and grew quiet, bowing from the waist.

My heart pumped with excitement, and the blood rushed in my

ears. The nobleman Ankh-hor had promised me the hunt of my life on the best hunting grounds in all Upper Egypt. At this moment on the Low Desert, Ra coming over the hills, nothing existed save the stench of the horse sweat and the baying of hounds. The wildness went straight to my head.

Maia had awakened me long before Ra began to glow on the horizon. She dressed me in a linen shift, looser than my normal gowns and not sheer at all. It covered my arms to the elbows. My sturdy sandals had only the slightest decoration; the lions tooled on the insoles said I vanquished the wild forces of the desert.

I chose the simplest jewelry, a gold chain necklace with small gold charms in the shape of crocodiles, vultures and rabbits. I would be aggressive like the crocodile, abundant as a rabbit and protected by the vulture. Gold wires with single amethyst teardrops went in my earlobes. The brilliant purple would ward off evil spirits.

The stones reminded me of the eunuch Qeb-ha's single amethyst ear drop, but I resisted all thought of him and his disapproval. *A high-priestess should not hunt; a high-priestess should not kill.* There were many things I did that a high-priestess shouldn't do. The plans of a god are one thing; the thoughts of men are another.

Still, I wore the Hathor lapis lazuli ring with golden horns on my right middle finger. The sacred ring was too precious for a wild day of chariots and lions, but the old priest Qeb-ha had unnerved me more than I admitted. I wanted protection from all sides.

"Welcome and Blessings, Isenkhebe Nefrusobek! I am Hetmus-hor, son of Ankh-hor, and honored to lead you in hunt on this most magnificent of days."

Hetmus-hor stood a head taller than the other men. He was as handsome as Tutankhamun and covered in as much gold. A white triangular headdress framed a bronzed face with a high-bridged straight nose and shining red-flecked brown eyes outlined in *kohl*. His dazzling smile flashed perfect white teeth.

He bent low and kissed the lapis ring on my hand. I could easily envision his broad shoulders wrestling a lion to the ground. I could easily imagine him wrestling me. When he straightened, my eyes were on level with his wide chest clad in an elaborate leather vest patterned in gold sunbursts. Ra coming over the mountains was not brighter than Hetmus-hor.

"You shall have my best charioteer," he announced. "My chariot will be in the lead. You shall follow directly behind with your Nubian in third position."

He still held my ringed hand when he lowered his voice and leaned so close that his speckled eyes were only inches away.

"If that is agreeable to you, Isis?" he asked with a hint of tease. His eyes twinkled when he said "Isis." He had the expression of a naughty boy delightfully testing his boundaries. He dared use my private name, and he knew me not at all. Hetmus-hor was indeed a confident man.

I pulled my hand back, but not in such a brusque manner as to discourage him. Only to rein him in a little. My eyes told him everything he needed to know.

"You move as fast as your chariot, Sir. Do not spend all your strength at the beginning of the hunt."

He laughed, a great booming sound, throwing his head back. It was all a game to him. He had been born to the hunt. There would be other moves. He looked forward to them with pleasure, as did I.

"By Horus, I love a woman with wit. If you hunt as well as you speak, we shall come home with enough trophies for another feast."

Never dimming his smile, he took my hand again to lead me to the shade of the sycamore grove.

"Bring wine," he called out. "Let us toast our honored guest, Isenkhebe Nefrusobek, who graces us with her beauty and intelligence."

He certainly knew how to flatter; he adapted his game quickly. He clearly noticed how his compliments to my wit pleased me. Charming words came easily to him. I had the feeling he had never struggled for anything in his life.

If the rumors the sloe-eyed woman whispered in my ear at last night's feast had any truth, he certainly never struggled to win a woman's favor.

"Hetmus-hor is as charming as a courtesan," she had confided with a knowing smile. *"He is quite known in Hermopolis for his powers of persuasion. There are more than a few wives and daughters who would attest that to be persuaded by Hetmus the Great Hunter is most pleasurable indeed."*

I had no objection to being persuaded; we clearly both wanted the same thing. I already envisioned us alone in the desert with the aroma of wild herbs in the hot air. I would twist my legs around his slim waist and hang from his broad shoulders. Then we would see if Hetmus the Hunter lived up to his reputation.

Servants appeared with tin goblets of unwatered Delta wine. The morning air was splendid in the crisp sunshine; there was no trace yet of the heat that would come.

Hetmus lifted his goblet to me and recited:

"May thou spend millions of years,
　　　　thou lover of Thebes,
Sitting with thy face to the north wind,
　　　　thy green eyes beholding felicity."

He had stolen the words of the ancient poem but substituted green eyes for me. I gave him the favor of a smile with a bold look that left the door wide open for possibilities.

"A toast to the kill!" a nobleman shouted.

Everyone, including the servants with the horses, cheered. I never felt more alive.

We flew across the sand and stone. I balanced on the rawhide flooring woven like strings on a tennis racket. Hares and wild dogs scattered when we passed. Herds of gazelle and oryx grazed until we thundered toward them, Berber dogs in the lead. Legs leaping through the air, horns high, the gazelle scattered to the winds.

I raised my prized bow, a composite of layers of wood, sinew and horn fashioned especially for me in Thebes. Its draw weight had been engineered for a woman's strength to bend the bow to full arrow length.

I let fly an arrow with a barbed bronze head designed to kill. It arched in the blue sky, then dropped with precision into the flank of a doe. She stumbled and fell. The dogs were upon her at once.

"Behkai! Abaqer!" Hetmus roared the names of the pack leaders, commanding them in Berber to back off.

They circled the fallen animal, snarling, tongues panting, saliva dripping in long strings. The other chariots gathered around, horses snorting and pawing the ground, anxious to run again. Dust swelled up in great clouds.

Hetmus pulled up beside me and extended his hand.

"It is your kill, Isis. It is the first kill of the day." His red-flecked eyes glowed with pride.

I stepped down from the chariot and walked with shaking knees toward the wounded doe thrashing on the ground. Hetmus-hor parted the snarling dogs with kicks and Berber barks, and I followed the path he blazed through the pack and the blood.

The female lay helpless, dark red flowed from her wound onto the golden sand. She turned her eyes toward me, big, brown and liquid.

"Come Isis, give thanks to the Goddess Neith and then put the animal out of her misery," Hetmus said.

His gentle tone surprised me; there was more to this nobleman than charm. He nodded his head slightly, his eyes saying, *You can do it.* Then he handed me a knife, but not my knife. I shook my head and drew my jeweled dagger from its tooled leather sheath.

After offering a silent prayer to Neith, the Goddess of Hunt, and another to Hathor, asking her forgiveness, I went to my knees, took the doe's muzzle in one hand and drew the steel blade deep across her throat, from ear to ear. A great gush of bright blood spewed onto my white gown. I felt both ill and elated. My hands trembled.

"Isenkhebe, Isenkhebe, Queen of the Hunt!" the men cheered.

The dogs howled at the scent of fresh blood, and Hetmus smacked one with his spear to keep him away.

My charioteer hauled the carcass onto our cart and draped her over the railing, the head flopping down toward the ground, blood still pouring from the wide gash. Her eyes were open but sightless and already drying in the heat. Flies swarmed in an instant from nowhere; they must be born from the very air.

Some blood dribbled from the flank wound and fell in droplets. Spots splashed on the tops of my feet and the hem of my caftan. The doe's heart no longer beat; the drops fell from the pull of gravity. By the time we returned to camp this afternoon, the animal would be bled.

The wind shifted suddenly and blew from the south with vengeance. Horses spooked and pulled at their reins; charioteers used all their strength to hold them in check. The hounds, lapping up blood-soaked sand, stopped and raised their noses, sniffing the charged air.

My gown whipped around my legs. I clutched the chariot rail for fear of blowing off, looking around frantically for something—anything—to protect my face from the biting sand. Holding on with my left hand, I bit the left sleeve of my gown and used my bloodied, jewelled dagger to saw off the cloth. In spite of the wind and the jolt of the chariot, I managed to wrap the linen around my nose and mouth.

I would have crouched down in the chariot, but there was just room for two to stand. My driver struggled with the horses; they reared up on their hind legs and pawed the air.

A brown wall was approaching, sweeping across the flat plateau as we stared. Hetmus shouted vainly into a wind that roared like ten thousand lions.

My driver pulled on the reins with all his strength. The white steeds at last put their hooves to the ground, but when they did, they bolted away from the camp in a desperate attempt to outrun the storm.

I hung on with both hands. The shouts faded behind us. The dead doe's head flopped wildly as we rolled over rocks and bounced high in the air. My driver never took his eyes from the backs of the horses and the treacherous ground ahead.

The wind became impossibly more vicious, and the sand enveloped us in a dense fog. I could no longer see the tails of the horses. Soon, I could not see the charioteer, who stood so close beside me that I felt his body movements in the thick dust.

He battled the horses and drove blind. We were thrown from side to side with such force that I would have flown from the cart, if not hanging on with both hands. I don't know how he could stand. The reins, taut in the pull between man and beasts, were his only anchor.

There was no time or space in the thick haze. I felt a great jolt and then we were flying, the wind swirling all around us. Had we been taken up into the sky?

We crashed in soft powder, and I was thrown from the chariot. I rolled, tumbling through a sea of sand, caught in swells as wild as any ocean tempest. I tried to stand up, but the force of the wind and sand kept me on my knees. The more I struggled, the deeper I sank.

I stretched out on my stomach, my head pointing away from the wind, my arms up to shield my head, the remaining sleeve of my dress for cover. The blowing sand cut my skin like a thousand shards of glass.

I could barely swallow through the dust in my throat. I pursed my lips, forcing myself to inhale through my nose not take more sand into my lungs. A person could drown in sand. I could be buried and never seen again.

The horses! Where were the horses? I could hear nothing but the howling wind. It went on for hours. Drowsiness overcame me. A hippo in soothing water swam by, but unlike my Abydos dream, she didn't offer me a ride.

Why hadn't I listened to Qeb-ha? Why hadn't I listened to my own heart? Even a fool acts wisely if he follows his heart.

"O Qeb-ha! Forgive me. I am a fool!"

My thoughts crawled through sand. My mind slowed to a standstill. A great silence engulfed me; I could no longer hear the wind. I was grateful. They say that silence conceals foolishness. I would hide and pray my fate would pass me by.

Chapter 13 Lion

I coughed once. Nasty brown phlegm came up. My eyes were dry and filled with grit. The weight of the sand lay heavy on my back and legs, but an air pocket around my head allowed me to breathe shallowly. I was careful not to gulp dust into my lungs.

My arms cramped from being in the same position so long, but I managed to use my hands to dig out a clear space to the surface. I could see daylight. Was it the same day, or had I slept through the night?

The sand weighed too much for me to rise. I pulled myself forward, like a snake slithering out of a hole. At last, I crawled free and rose numbly to my knees. There was nothing around me except sand and the high sides of a *wadi*, a dry river bed now filled with golden dust.

My skin raw and chaffed red from the blasting sand was on fire. But I lived. My caftan, once snowy white, was filthy. Brown dust had settled in the fibers of the weave; a dark splotch covered the bodice. Blood. The jewelled dagger cutting deep across the doe's throat seemed a lifetime ago.

The chariot had to be close. Had the driver survived? I saw no sign of the horses. Could creatures so big be buried out of sight? Nothing in the sand indicated that a horse or chariot was entombed beneath the surface.

I crawled on my knees in what I hoped was the direction of the chariot. I was unbearably thirsty; my tongue swelled and filled my whole mouth. My lips were cracked. When I tried to moisten them, no saliva came. The desert had tried to suck the life from me, but still I breathed.

My knee banged against something hard; I felt the shaft of the chariot. It must be standing on its end. The horses had simply disappeared. I couldn't bear the thought of being alone and clawed at the sand in a state of near hysteria.

My hunting dagger with jeweled hilt was still tied around my hips, but my bow and arrow must be buried with the chariot. Water! The chariot carried goatskins of water for a day of hunt. I dug and dug and never looked around.

They were on me without warning. One came up behind and grabbed me by the waist, just as I saw his shadow on the ground. I screamed, and my fear echoed off the rock walls of the dry river bed.

We struggled in the sand; my attacker kept sinking deeper. I fought as hard as I could, but was no match at all. One grabbed my feet, and another my shoulders, dragging me between them as they stumbled for footing.

Finally at the top of the ridge, they dropped me onto the rocky ground. They were angry, red in the face, hot from exertion, and humiliated that a woman could have caused them so much trouble. One kicked me in the side with his foot encased in a heavy sandal that laced up his shin.

"Stop! She's no good to us dead or broken."

A harsh voice. I recognized the guttural words of Aramaic.

A man pulled me to my feet, and I stared straight at a golden lion insignia with massive legs and curled mane. The Lion of Persia! How could Persians be here, so close to the Nile?

A soldier threw a filthy, coarse wool cape over my head and tossed me onto a horse. I hung upside down, belly across the felted pads used as saddle. I saw the doe draped across my chariot, her head bouncing as we rolled across the desert. This was swift justice from the Goddess.

The rider mounted behind me, and the horses thundered off. I couldn't tell in which direction, but felt certain they would not head west toward the Nile.

What of Hetmus-hor? Had he made it out alive? And my slave Goliath? Had he lost his life to follow me on this folly? Or did they already search for me? Would they come, but too late?

I lost track of time, but don't think we traveled that far before we stopped. Feet, belonging to man and horse, were all I could see.

I was so thirsty. I had never imagined such a thirst; the pain was beyond bearing. I would sell my soul for a sip of water.

Rough hands dragged me from the horse and threw me over a shoulder. I had no strength left to struggle. We were in a camp; I could tell by the sounds, but couldn't see much beyond the dusty ground. The earth had been churned up in a mad pattern of footprints and horse hooves.

We swept through wool panels into a tent, where I was tossed down on thick carpets like a sack of old rags. My captor prostrated himself beside me.

"What is this?"

The rough voice was more growl of a beast than man, but the Aramaic was clean; I guessed an educated man. I thanked my father for my language tutors. I was terrified, but at least I understood what was being said.

"We found her in the desert, General, after the Great Storm. She was alone, her chariot and horses buried in the sand."

"Idiots!" The General's voice was deafening. "Why did you not leave her there to die?"

The prostrate man beside me kept his face buried in the carpet. I could see his trembling hands out of the corner of my eye.

"Show her to me."

A rough hand grabbed my arm and dragged me to my feet. The foul-smelling cape was pulled away, and I stood as straight as I could, considering the beating my body had taken. Every muscle screamed from bruise and dehydration.

I faced six standing men around a wooden table covered with scrolls. They were all of the same build, stocky and powerful, with the muscles of oxen. Their calves looked as big around as my waist. They wore their hair in shoulder-length plaits entwined with colorful ribbons; their beards were carefully groomed into long curls.

Leather military waistcoats, armored with metal mesh and emblazoned with the golden lion of Persia, covered their massive chests. I could tell by their bearing these men were high-born. This was no small raiding party.

An ogre with bulging eyes and thick lips moved so close to me, I smelled his foul breath and the sweat under his perfume. He appraised me from head to foot, like a man in a brothel before making his choice.

"She is no ordinary Egyptian, my General. Look at her jewelry. There could be a fine ransom here."

"Idiots!" The General roared even louder. "If she is a woman of importance, do you not think they will be searching for her? Do you suppose she was in the desert by herself, driving her own chariot?"

More than one man quivered.

The General himself came to stand just in front of me. When he fingered the necklace of gold charms and lifted a tiny crocodile, his hand grazed my chest, and my skin crawled. But I knew his character by that choice of the crocodile. This was a man who lusted, and not only for power.

I forced myself not to flinch, but stood immobile, concentrating on breathing slowly, ignoring my racing heart.

"Well, she is here now. There is no changing that." His voice changed; he studied me from under half-closed lids.

"They will be looking for her. Place extra guards. Follow the tracks backwards and erase them. Post men five miles down the ravine toward the southwest."

Three men left the tent immediately.

"You made an unwise decision," the General growled at the prostrated man without taking his eyes from mine. "You have endangered the mission."

I stared back, determined not to blink or show fear.

"But perhaps these emerald eyes bewitched you. I shall decide your fate when I decide hers."

The man beside me slithered forward on his stomach and kissed the General's feet. My green eyes had saved his life for the moment— and mine.

"Get her cleaned up. Get her out of those rags. Feed her." He turned his back and returned to the scrolls.

They were not going to kill me, at least not right away. He would not have ordered me to be fed. I had no idea how much time had passed since I had eaten, but I could not feel hunger when my need for water was so desperate. A person can live a long time without food, but without water, the desert sun can suck the life from you in one day.

Three women came to me when I entered the tent. The guard grunted instructions about bathing and food, and then turned and exited without a glance back.

They touched the soft linen of my spoiled gown and rubbed it between their fingers to appreciate the delicate texture. They removed my wig and passed it around, fingering each golden trinket. A slant-eyed young girl hardly more than a child put a small piece between her teeth and bit down. Her eyes grew wide when she recognized gold. They toyed with the amethysts hanging from my ears, shrieking when they realized they were not glass.

A servant brought water at last, and I gulped it down so quickly that it came right up again. The next time I sipped slowly, taking small swallows with time in between to settle. I began to feel human again. I told myself that I would survive even this.

I didn't let myself think about how I would get home—really home, back to Las Vegas, back to Barb, back to the 21st century. I vowed if I ever got home again, I would get rid of the Red Mirror.

I hurt everywhere. Purple bruises from the struggle at the chariot marked my raw skin. It would take days to heal, but I didn't know if I had days. I didn't know if I had hours.

Boiling water flowed from brass jugs into great copper basins. The women sponged me from the crown of my shaved head down to my henna-tipped toes. They wore their own hair. How did they keep clean and free from vermin in these stuffy tents with no bathing pools?

They oiled my bruised body; my skin soaked it up like a sponge. They polished my nails with a pumice stone, smoothing out the broken edges. My beautiful hands! Cut and blistered raw. Gold gleamed from the horns in the ring that matched my mother Sit-hathor's, one of only two in all Egypt. It gave me strength to see it on my middle finger, a reminder that I was Isenkhebe Nefrusobek, High Priestess of Hathor.

Finally, I was clean, oiled and perfumed. They brought me a splendid robe of floral-patterned yellow silk. But even it was painful against my skin; I shuddered when they slipped it around my shoulders. A long sash with golden tassels and tinkling bells went around my waist.

The girl with slanted eyes and high cheekbones put delicate slippers on my feet, curled-up toes in front, open in the back. They had been woven from thousands of red silk threads.

The hot tea was very sweet, generous with honey. A platter appeared with rice and mutton stewed with figs and raisins. I choked down the meat. No Egyptian of status ever ate the flesh of a goat.

After I ate and drank, they brought me a small pipe with sweet smoke. I drew one deep breath, coughed and pushed the pipe away. My eyes drooped. I floated above the rich carpets and drifted between the poles of the tent.

A rough, guttural voice broke through the trance, and two men in leather vests with curved daggers in their belts stood over me.

"Come," they growled in a crude Aramaic and hauled me to my feet.

Chapter 14 Ishtar

"On your face, Egyptian whore, before the great General Sher, lion of the desert and beloved of Cambyses, King of the World."

The guards pushed me first to my knees and then my face into the dusty rug. The General reclined on cushions, his uniform replaced with a robe, silk like mine, but deep green.

"Bring her up to her knees. Let us see her face washed of desert filth and tears."

They pulled me to rest on my haunches, the gown flowing around me, shimmering gold in the yellow of the oil lamps. The women had cleaned my wig and covered it with a long scarf of emerald silk, woven with gold thread in an intricate arabesque pattern. It cascaded around my shoulders in stark contrast to the yellow of the robe. My amethyst earrings dangled from my earlobes.

The same officers were there and still in uniform. They stood while the General lounged. Unlike Egyptians, the *kohl* around their eyes was drawn to make them appear perfectly round. They stared at me. I didn't need a mirror to tell me how I looked. I saw it clearly by the lust in their eyes. But I saw hatred, too.

They talked to each other without looking away from my face. They spoke Elamite-Persian, not the Aramaic of the soldiers. I understood it well enough to hear them discuss if I should be killed now and taken down to the plain and dumped. They reasoned that a search party would find me and take my body home. They would have time to finish their mission for Cambyses.

The General rose from his seat. The others fell silent. He loomed over me, a great bull with a massive chest and legs like the thick columns of a temple. I looked up into his eyes and saw a slight spark of something human. I stared straight at him and refused to blink.

Seconds passed. No one spoke or moved. The wicks in the lamps spluttered, making small hissing sounds like a thousand serpents.

"Leave us."

It was all he said. He never took his eyes away. We had locked into battle; he was not accustomed to defeat.

When the last man had exited, his face relaxed just a fraction; an ironic smile curved his lips. He stared at me still but with less intensity.

It was he who turned away first. He reached for a goblet on a brass tray set on a short wooden tripod and sank again onto his cushions, contemplating me from across the carpets.

"I shall call you *Ishtar*," he said idly in Persian. "You are the glittering evening star in a lavender desert sky."

"I am worth much to my people." My voice rang out strong and clear in the small space of the tent; it reflected none of the terror I felt. "They will pay well for my safe return."

The General sputtered into the wine cup he held to his lips; he looked stunned.

"You speak Aramaic? But are you not Egyptian?"

"I am from Thebes, your Excellency, but speak several tongues." I would not let him know I understood Persian, the private language of noblemen.

I thought it wise to use a title of respect. This man held my life in his thick fingers. He studied me for a few long, silent moments. His thick eyelids drooped. He sipped from his goblet with his thick meaty lips. I was deciding if I dared speak again when his eye went to my hand.

"What does it mean that you wear the ring of the Goddess of Love?"

"Hathor is more than the Goddess of Love, esteemed General," I answered, hoping to convince him of my importance. "She is the Solar Goddess, the Gold-of-the-Gods."

His face turned hard in an instant; his upper lip curled, exposing yellowed, square teeth, big and strong enough to grind raw flesh.

"Do not presume to instruct me about the inferior gods of Egyptian dogs," he snarled. "Why do you wear the ring?"

This man needed the most delicate of handling. He would have no patience with word games but might respond to directness.

"I am a high priestess in the cult of Hathor. I assure you the Temple will pay whatever you demand for my return, safe and untouched."

"And if you are *touched*?"

I hated the amused smirk on his face.

"What then, High Priestess of Hathor?"

I didn't answer but met his eyes directly, unflinching. There was no amusement on my side.

Morphing before me again, his eyes went cold and soulless with the steady stare of a predator. The General was a chameleon, a hybrid of bull and lion, with only occasional glimpses of man.

"I am not in need of a ransom from effeminate Nile priests." His voice was as frigid as a winter wind.

He sipped his wine, studying me over the rim of the goblet. He waited for my response. Everything depended on the next moment—my future and my life.

"Could it be possible for a lion of Persia to have needs not met?" My voice was both coy and bold with the tease of promise.

I saw his pupils dilate, even surrounded by his coal black iris. His eyelids jerked slightly; I had touched a nerve. He tried to keep his face stone, but revealed all in the blink of his eye. No matter his words, he was a man of many needs, some never met.

The General sipped from his goblet and drew smoke from his

pipe. I smelled the same sweet odor as in the women's tent.

"I have a proposal for you, Ishtar," he said as casually as if he invited me to tea.

"I sense you like challenge. I hear that certain priestesses of Hathor have—what shall we say?—exceptional talents. Your reputation reaches as far as Persia."

He hesitated only long enough to gauge my reaction. I showed him nothing.

"If you please me, you will belong to me and me alone, but only as long as I am pleased. When you no longer please, I shall return you to the women's tent, where you can please the other men. And when you please them no more, I shall have you killed."

I watched his lips move in his impassive face. How easily he talked about my inevitable death. It had been decided; it was only a question of when.

"But because you are a high priestess, I shall return your body to the temple, so that the priests can mummify you, and you can live forever in your Egyptian dream of eternity."

Silence.

"What do you say to that, Ishtar?"

Not more than one minute passed. Instead of answering, I rose from my knees to my feet in one movement. I no longer felt the pain in my body. I moved slowly toward him. The emerald scarf slipped from my head to the carpet; the gold in my black wig glittered. The bells on my sash jingled seductively, like the tinkle of the *sistrum* in the temple.

I fixed my eyes on his and knelt at his feet. I took the goblet from his hand and placed it on the brass tray beside his cushions.

They teach in the temple that there is a sexual power inside us that when summoned, oozes from our pores. It's an animal energy that conjures up base desire. But the magic of Hathor is special; it transforms raw lust into a promise of pleasure and satisfaction known only by the gods.

I turned on the Power. My body radiated animal sex mingled

with the potent allure of intense sensuality—and deep mystery.

"I have secrets," my aura teased, "wonderful secrets that only I can share."

Electricity sparked in the air. Great sensuous waves rolled over the General. Mesmerized, he barely breathed; his eyes fixed on my every movement.

I slowly untied the purple silk sash of his robe. I pulled it free in one long motion and dropped it carefully next to the pillows. His eyes blinked when he felt its slick slide across the small of his back. I opened the front of his gown, folding the cloth back without hurry. I never took my eyes from his. His breathing came shallow and fast.

He was nude under the robe. I let my eyes wander. I caressed him with only my gaze, appreciating the muscles of his broad chest, the mass of thick, curly hair, like a beast. His nipples were already erect. I looked long at each one, but did not touch him.

I followed the line of hair down his hard belly. It crossed his navel and descended into a great black bush. His thighs were thick tree trunks. His manhood stood erect and hard, an obelisk to the sky. It looked as thick as my fist. I leaned back on my heels to study him. My eyes followed the vein down the underside to the huge swollen sacks at its base. The man was truly a bull.

I started with the sacks. I took one in my mouth while I gripped the other in my hand—hard. The General gave an involuntary cry. I sucked harder and gripped harder. The rougher my touch, the more he moaned.

When I felt him near the edge, I stopped and traced my tongue up the vein. I massaged his balls gently, a new caress, light and ethereal. When I arrived at the head, I eased his foreskin down with my fingers. I pulled harder and harder, the glossy bulb erupting out with each downward tug. I could see the skin stretching almost to breaking point; small droplets of clear liquid bubbled from the tip.

I pumped him up and down, up and down, while squeezing his shaft in my fist. The rhythm was steady. He thrust his hips for me to go faster, but I stayed in control. I took my time, tormenting him with his own urgency.

I slowed and put my tongue to the head, exploring the surface, licking its smoothness, biting with my sharp teeth. I stuck the pointed tip of my tongue into the small opening there. One hand held the shaft; the other was back on his balls, pulling and kneading, first rough, then gentle, then rough again. As full as his sacks were, I managed to have both in one hand.

The General twisted and panted. Each time he came close to exploding, I stopped. How many times could I bring him to the edge before I let him go over?

Putting my knees between his thighs, I forced them apart. I lowered my open mouth onto his manhood and took him in as far as I could. I sucked him with all my strength. I rocked him hard, my hands on his hips to give me more force, his shaft thrusting deep into my throat.

And then when I sensed he was just there, I pinched his erect nipple hard and put my finger at the lip of his anus and plunged in.

He erupted with a great shaking and bolting like a wild horse. I held on to him, my finger in his anus, twisting his nipple without mercy, his manhood filling my mouth until he collapsed and breathed in great gulps.

He had never touched me, except to hold my head when I sucked him. I had never opened my robe. He lay spent, his massive chest rising high and falling. I rolled back on my haunches and to my feet to stand over him. I said nothing.

The General opened his eyes, looking up at me. There was something new there. Just a flicker, but it was a start.

Reaching down slowly, I folded his robe across his bare chest and loins. I handed him his goblet of wine and stepped backwards, folding to my knees again on the carpet, in front of him. Not one word had been spoken since his life-and-death challenge to me.

I waited. I looked straight at him, unblinking. I believe my face was expressionless. I tried hard that it was. Inside I quaked. I had given it everything I had.

Shouting outside of the tent broke the spell. A guard called out, begging permission to enter. The General jumped to his feet and tied the sash around his waist.

"Enter," he roared. "This had better be good!"

A captain prostrated himself at the General's monster feet.

"Speak, damn you, why do you keep me waiting?"

"The outward guards have spotted Egyptian chariots, Excellency. They camp for the night."

The General was instantly alert.

"How many? How far away?"

"Eight, sir. They are not military. They have not entered the canyon area."

"A search party. It is just as I said. They are looking for her."

He paced back and forth.

"Have you covered our tracks?"

"Yes, Excellency. The trail is wiped out."

"Keep watching them. Do not let them see you. If they do not find the trail, they will turn back. If they discover the trail, kill them all and bury the chariots. They must not see us and live to tell." His eyes flashed with cold fire.

"But, hear this," he threatened. "I do not desire more Egyptians disappearing into the desert. We cannot have their army join the search. Our work is not finished here."

He was fully in command; it seemed not passion nor fury clouded his thinking. I could see why he was so respected and feared.

"Call my staff and have them here at once."

"Yes, General. At once."

"All this for a woman!" he fumed. "Damn the Gods."

His aura was black and evil. I despaired that all my efforts were for naught.

He turned on me. Would he kill me right here, right now? The flush on his angry face faded slightly. When he spoke, his voice was almost human.

"You have gained yourself a night, Ishtar. The reputation of

Hathor is well deserved." A tiny spark of delight twinkled in his eyes. "Maybe even more than could be imagined."

He started to dress.

"Go to the harem and sleep. No one will approach you."

A soldier appeared to take me to the women's tent, but not before I saw something glint on the table. It was the jewel-encrusted hilt of my dagger.

Chapter 15 The Sash

Would this be the last dawn of my life in this world? A soldier shook my shoulder and barked for me to get up. I still had on the yellow gown, my wig on my head. Sleep had taken me the moment I lay down, and if I journeyed to the land of dreams, I was too exhausted to notice.

He took me to a place to relieve myself and finally I could see the camp. Tents formed regular rows in a narrow canyon with steep walls. You could only approach from one direction. The horses were tethered in one spot, outside the camp perimeter at the mouth of the ravine. I saw only one guard posted there.

The General's tent stood apart from the others with its back up to the canyon wall. Deep tracks carved by erosion etched the cliff surface. When I looked more closely, I spotted small trails at a much shallower slope; they could be the paths of mountain goats or maybe shepherds. Bedouins lived in these rocky hills.

When we came to the General's tent, the guard pushed me roughly through the flap. I immediately prostrated myself. I didn't want my face shoved into the dusty carpet again.

I came to my knees and faced the General.

He was drinking hot liquid from a ceramic cup, his massive feet clad in heavy sandals propped on a cushion. He had on his leather tunic with a short kilt. Did the man ever sleep?

More of the rice and a pile of dates filled the platter in front of him. I was ravenous and thirsty. He saw me glance at the food.

"Come, eat, drink." He motioned me over with a dismissive wave of his hand.

With the practiced grace of a dancer, I rose from my knees to my feet and then settled again on the opposite side of the dish. He handed me a cup filled with honey-sweetened tea. I smelled mint. It was too hot to swallow more than small sips.

I fought to control my urge to down it all at once.

He watched me, detached, as if observing a prized mare feeding in the stable. I scooped up rice with my right hand, and using my fingers and palm to craft a small ball, put it in my mouth. I willed myself to chew. My hunger was like a dog; I could have swallowed each chunk whole.

"Persians never eat with women. Did you know that, Ishtar? But you are Egyptian. I am curious to see if you are different."

I had no comment. What could I say? How many ways are there to eat?

"Women must chatter while they chew. They cannot be silent. It is distasteful to see."

I was silent.

"Perhaps you are different, after all. I sense your mind working, but your lips are still. Would I dread your words, Ishtar, if I could hear them?"

I had no idea where he was going with this line of conversation. I continued to eat and looked at him only when he spoke. I took a date and nibbled around the pit, then drank deep of my tea, which had cooled.

"My officers want me to kill you, Ishtar. They say you are endangering the mission. What do you say to that?"

His tone was lazy, as if he casually mused over the fate of a goat.

Still I didn't speak. Did he want me to beg for my life? Would that elicit pleasure—or scorn? One should not give way to the tongue when not asked. I would not give way to my tongue, until I knew *why* I had been asked.

He continued in the same casual tone.

"I told them that it would be a pity to destroy such a creature as you. But then, they do not know you as I do."

He waited. He expected a response. I had to gamble. I had no choice. I modulated my voice carefully in a tone confident with the hint of challenge.

"You told me that I would be yours as long as I pleased you. Have I not pleased you? Or are you not a man of your word?"

He actually laughed. He threw back his head and gave a mighty roar of a laugh. He smiled at me. I saw his strong, yellow-stained teeth. His eyes crinkled in the corners.

"I am certain, Ishtar, that there are few men you would not please."

He refilled his cup and mine and settled back; he appeared utterly at ease.

"I value beauty, and I value brains, but I value talent most of all. And you, beautiful and clever Ishtar, have been given an extraordinary talent. It would be a crime to waste it."

For the first time I thanked my mother for developing my special abilities with all the skills of her cult. My father had given me language, so I could understand and spar. And of course, I thanked Hathor for giving me the Power. I owed my life today to all three.

I waited for a signal, a sign of what he wanted next. He wouldn't tell me, of course. He played the cat to my mouse. He wanted me to squirm, and then he would pounce with his great paw when he was ready.

The General watched me, never taking his eyes away. I looked all around the tent. Neither of us spoke, each waiting to see what the other would do. I saw a whip—the kind Persians use on horses—on top of a pile with saddle pads and a bridle.

I moved the tray of food between us to one side. His pupils

dilated. He stopped smiling. I stood up before him and untied the sash of my robe. The gown fell open in front, not all the way, but enough that he could see the curve of my belly, my shaven mound, and a hint of my breast. Taking the sash in my hand, I doubled it, forming a loop.

As fast as a striking cobra, I slipped the loop around his neck and yanked hard. I caught him totally off guard. The little bells tinkled; the tassels swung back and forth. He went wide-eyed with shock. I released the pressure so he could breathe.

"You go too far!" He bellowed like a bull.

My voice cut through the air.

"I have not begun."

I held onto the end of the noose with one hand and reached for the whip with the other. My robe fell open when I stretched, revealing my full breasts, crowned with dusky roses and tightened nipples. He didn't try to remove the sash from around his throat.

Gripping the whip, I lashed him across his biceps; the leather thongs stung his flesh. I jerked hard at the noose at the same time.

A great moan heaved from his bull chest. His manhood rose under the kilt. I lashed him again, on the other arm, harder this time. Angry red welts came up on his skin. His erection grew larger still.

I whipped his thighs, still tightening and releasing the noose with each stroke. He snorted like a wild bull. I expected him to rise up and paw the ground.

I only struck a half dozen times, but each blow was more forceful than the one before. He grabbed the whip with one hand and seized my hand holding the noose with his other. He pulled me on top of him, my soft breasts crushing into the stiff leather of his vest, the metal lions and mesh imprinting a pattern on my skin.

He flipped me forward on my knees like I was a loaf of bread and dragged me backward. I felt his massive rod ram deep into me. Thank Horus, he had chosen the canal of my womanhood and not the other. I feared I would split apart. Could I survive such a weapon?

But he exploded the moment he entered me. He lost control.

He held my hips flush against his groin and breathed hard like a runner after a race. Then he released me, shoving me face down on my stomach while he fell back onto the cushions.

I could see through a crack at the base of the tent that Ra had vanquished the serpent of the underworld and begun once again his journey across the sky. I wondered again if this was the last sunrise I would see.

The women bathed me and dressed me in new gowns. The first layer was a blue-green caftan, the color of Sinai turquoise, with elaborate embroidery in gold around the neck, cuff, and hemline. Over that they placed a delicate open robe in a rich lapis blue.

Persian women always cover their hair. They chose for me pale lavender silk with thousands of shimmering silver threads. When they brought more slippers with turned-up toes, I asked for sandals.

They looked at each other and shrugged; the one with slanted eyes came back with Persian leather sandals that laced up the leg. I took them into the folds of my gown and put the slippers on my feet. They watched me but said nothing. I hated looking into their empty eyes; I could not see their souls.

A guard came for me, and I returned to the General's tent. The officers were all there, very animated, gesturing wildly with their hands. Rumor told that Persians drink copious amounts of wine when making decisions, but wait until they are sober to act. I prayed to Hathor they would not act now.

The men fell silent when I entered and prostrated myself. Hatred sucked the air from the tent. They needed only a word from the General to slit my throat right there on the rug.

"Go to the bed," he commanded, not even looking in my direction.

I rose and went to the mattress with silk pillows and settled myself on my knees. Conscious of each movement in my body, I did everything to suppress the Power. This was not the time. My eyes avoided the group of staring men; I tried to fade into the patterns and shadows of the tent.

They soon forgot me and spoke rapidly, some of it military jargon, words I didn't know. But I understood "supply lines" and "direction of attack." They talked freely in Persian, unaware I could follow, outlining the weakness of Egyptian defenses and mocking the ailing Pharaoh and his son, Crown Prince Psamtik.

It is a gift from the gods, they said, for such a weakling as Psamtik to face Cambyses, the Master of All Lands. They spoke of invasion and the King of Persia as the next Pharaoh; Egyptian power was at an end. Persian gods, superior to the weak gods of the Nile, would rule a new world.

My fear grew with each moment, but I feigned a look of boredom as I picked at the threads of my dress. Images of peaceful Nile temples with green fields and lush gardens played in my mind. I saw them invaded and trampled by these beast-men with perfumed beards and icy hearts.

Worry and fear overwhelmed my desire to remain strong. I began to think of dying as preferable to this unknowing. When worry such as mine arises, the heart seeks death itself as escape. Still I was jolted when I heard them switch to talk of killing me.

Their eyes pierced me like twelve deadly daggers. I forced myself to stare at the golden threads frayed by my nervous picking.

The General ended the discussion.

"Enough. It is for me to decide. When the time is right, I shall act."

Again I could feel the hatred, palpable in the heat of the stuffy tent. Did these people ever need fresh air?

The language switched to Aramaic when a captain appeared with a report.

"The Egyptians are on foot, your Excellency, exploring the canyons. There is no sign of reinforcements."

"They do not take their horses? Then they are low on water."

The General tapped a whip against his thigh. It was the same whip I had used on him in the morning.

"But reinforcements are coming, of that I am certain. They do not leave. They expect more men and supplies."

He fell silent. No one else spoke. I ventured a look in his direction from under my lashes. He stared at me, but I couldn't read his face.

"Bring my horse," he ordered. "I want to see for myself. And bring the woman whatever she needs. I want her here when I return."

It wasn't until he left that I realized I had been holding my breath.

I was alone in the tent. I waited a few moments, then rose to my feet and went to the table. Some of the papyri were maps, but I also saw long lists and official-looking documents. I moved aside a scroll to uncover my jeweled hunting knife.

After putting the dagger in the folds of my robe, I replaced the scroll exactly where it had been. The table looked undisturbed. I hurried back to the bed and hid the knife with the Persian sandals.

I was on my way to the back of the tent when the guard entered with a platter of rice, some meat and a water jug.

"Do you have any bread?" My voice showed no fear.

He looked surprised; he wasn't used to women or prisoners asking for anything. But he returned with a flat, round loaf of dark bread, the kind Bedouins bake in the sand under a campfire.

The bread went with my knife and sandals. The green scarf from last night had fallen between two pillows; I added it to the hidden pile.

I had no real plan. I moved on automatic. The only way out of the camp was past the horses, through the narrow canyon mouth. It was bright day, with soldiers everywhere.

One of the tent flaps in the back toward the cliff wall was not staked to the ground. The wind must have loosened it. I went to my knees and lifted a corner; bright light poured into the dim interior. The cliff wall was about six feet away. I saw no guards; they stood round in front.

I forced myself to eat the food, choking down the foul mutton, drinking some of the water. A small stack of goatskin water bags was neatly arranged not far from the table of scrolls. I took one from the middle of the stack and filled it with the remaining water from the jug. I put that with my secret stash and went back to the bed to await the General's return.

Chapter 16   The Bite

Covered in dust and stinking like a stable, the General stomped into the tent, his hungry eyes searching for me. I looked for my death sentence in his face, but if he had decided I must die, I couldn't see it there. He hurried toward me, shedding his armor with each step.

"You smell like a horse," I said calmly. My strength came from somewhere outside me. Inside, I quaked from anxiety and fear.

He stopped short—speechless, his leather vest half on, half off.

I relaxed on one elbow, slightly on my side, accentuating the curve from my shoulder to narrow waist that rose again along my hip. My legs stretched out, ankles resting gracefully one on the other, knee slightly bent, toes pointed. The blue silk folded on every contour of my body. I stared at him boldly from under half-closed lids and dialed up the Power.

"Water!" He bellowed through the closed flap. "Bring me water for a bath. And food."

He pulled off his thick sandals and tossed them aside, standing in his loose shirt and kilt. Sweat made rivulets in the pale powder on his skin. Stripes from my whip flamed bright red on his arms and legs. I wondered what his men thought when they saw those.

Pots clanged and voices rose as the camp prepared for the evening meal. Ra was retreating under the western horizon. Other night sounds echoed through the canyon, subtle but different vibrations that went with the changes of texture in the late evening air. I felt it slightly cooler in the stifling tent.

The General grabbed a jug of water and poured a stream down his throat. It spilled into his beard, caked with dust. Why don't Persians shave like civilized people? All that hair was so unclean.

The food arrived first. He sat on cushions in his dirty shirt and kilt, stuffing slabs of fatty meat into his mouth. Bits of it clung to his beard. And he says it's distasteful to eat with women who chatter while they chew.

I saw him as raw animal. I envisioned him returning from battle, covered in human blood, ravenous for the taste of rare meat.

Twilight had settled when they brought the steaming bath water in brass jugs with large copper bowls. Stacks of coarse cloth arrived with it. Small decorated beakers of perfumed oil stood on a round brass tray.

"Do you wish me to bathe you?" I asked politely.

"Do you see anyone else here?" His voice was gruff, but not threatening.

I took several lengths of the cloth and spread them over cushions.

"Lie here," I told him.

He called the guard.

"Do not disturb me. Do not enter unless there is news of the Egyptians."

The guard fixed on the General when he spoke, but I could tell he looked at me out of the corner of his eye. I wondered what camp gossip whispered about me. There must be wild speculation about the Egyptian sorceress who had bewitched their General.

The General settled on the cushions, his massive frame bending with a grace I wouldn't have thought possible in a man his size.

I pulled his shirt over his head and put it aside. Then I removed his kilt and put it on top. He was already erect, but I ignored it.

Beginning with his arms, I wiped the layers of dust away. I moved to his thighs and stroked downward to his calves and ankles, dipping the cloth from time to time in water. When the cloth became too brown, I took a clean one. When the water became brown, I poured fresh.

I rinsed his hair and long beard and wiped the grime from his face. I washed his feet, and between his toes. I bathed him as I would a small child. I did not turn on the Power.

His body relaxed, the erection melted. He closed his eyes and I thought him asleep. But when I started to move away, he opened them and asked, "Where are you going?"

"To get more towels and the oil, Excellency."

I dribbled scented oil into fresh water and swabbed his entire body, now clean of dust and sweat. Only when I gently washed his testicles and penis, did the erection come back.

It had to be dark now. The lamps in the tent gave off a mellow glow. I could hear the camp laughing around the cooking fires, eating the evening meal, enjoying the soft night after a fierce day.

When finished, I took away the jugs and the dirty cloths and put some clean fabric by the bed. The General lay with his eyes closed, relaxed. I brought him his pipe with the sweet smelling smoke and lit it for him. He leaned up against the pillows and drew deep drafts; the muscles in his face calmed even more. He was quite handsome really, in a brutish way.

I slid out of my robe and pulled the caftan over my head; both tumbled to a lush pile. Deliberately, slowly, I straddled him, unhurriedly stretching forward, only the tips of my erect nipples grazing his flesh. I took my time to slither from the black bush nesting his stallion manhood, past his thick waist, to his gorilla chest.

I kissed him deep and caring, my tongue probing the inside of his mouth. No urgency, just languid, very tranquil. The last hint of tension in his massive bulk evaporated into me, and then flowed through me into the thick, hazy air.

My nude body lay full on top of him. The warmth of his skin

burned into mine; the beat of his heart reverberated into my chest. My lips pressed softly on his again. He floated up from the cushions.

I kissed him on his broad chest, everywhere, in a language that said, "I adore you." I kissed the red welts on his arms. I kissed his hands and put them to my breasts. He squeezed me, but gently. Expecting pain, I got tenderness.

His hands moved up and down my body; he stroked me, his palms rough and calloused. My skin, still chaffed from the blasting sand, was velvet compared to his battle-worn flesh.

I whispered in his ear, "Let us go to the bed."

He picked me up while still reclining and then stood. My feet dangled in the air. He kissed me as he lay me down. The power and sensibility of it surprised me. I was breathless. He began to make love to me, not animal sex, but a kind of raw passion with tender emotion that moved me.

I stirred; I couldn't help myself. He was overwhelming me.

I stretched my neck so that he would find the trigger points that ignite my fire. He found them. He found them all, and he tasted them all with his wet lips, broad tongue, and sometimes his teeth.

It was building in me. I didn't want to believe it, but I was so wet that the damp was on the inside of my thighs. My nipples were rock hard and pointed. Animal sounds rumbled deep in my throat like the low growls of a lioness.

No more touching. My hand found his stone pedestal, so thick I could scarcely close my fingers around it. I guided him to me and placed him at the gate. He moved his hips slowly and probed a little deeper with each thrust.

My juices flowed so that even he, in his great size, was gliding with ease. He filled me and stretched me, and still I wanted more. I couldn't get enough of him inside me. When he lunged into me, my hips rose to meet him. I hung onto his broad neck while he pounded me amid cries of pleasure, his and mine.

"Deeper," I pleaded. "Deeper!"

My words electrified him. He came to his knees, lifting me with him. He had the strength of ten bulls. He stretched his legs out and held me in his lap with his Min manhood so deep in me that it crushed against the tip of my womb.

My legs locked around his hips. My own weight pushed my swollen bud against his iron shaft.

He rocked me back and forth, and I could only hang my head backwards and plead for mercy. But when he slowed, I begged for more.

When I could bear it no longer, a comet erupted up through my cervix and out the crown of my head. I soared to the heavens.

Contraction after contraction pulsed in my womb. It went on forever; I wanted it to go on forever. I held onto his massive arms, my nails digging in his flesh. I would not let go.

He lay me down and moved inside me, slowly. All the way in, and then almost out, before sliding deep again. I stopped swirling and came back to earth. I reached between his legs and took his sacks in my hand, squeezing with each thrust. I stretched for his neck with my lips, and he lowered himself.

I bit him in that place that is my own trigger point. I tasted a drop of blood.

It was the bite that brought him over. His body convulsed; a long, protracted howl escaped his throat. I feared the guards would come, but they didn't. They knew now was no time to enter.

He collapsed on top of me, struggling to catch his breath.

"You are too heavy. I cannot breathe," I whispered into his chest.

He rolled off me and lay spread-eagle on the bed. His eyes closed. His massive chest rose and fell. His manhood lay limp against his thigh.

The jeweled hilt of the dagger was cool to my hand. I didn't think; I didn't hesitate. I grabbed his beard and plunged the blade deep, drawing it across his throat from ear to ear, just like the doe. It took all my strength.

My hand found the green silk scarf, the one that matched my eyes, and I stuffed it in the gaping hole. He choked. His eyes were immense and bewildered. He looked at me in utter disbelief.

"I'm sorry," I whispered to his lips quivering in death throe. "I'm so sorry, but you would never have let me go."

I covered his nude dying body with a blanket. I wanted to dress him but didn't dare take the time.

Grabbing the sandals, I tied them to my feet, my fingers shaking so hard I could barely hold the thongs. After pulling the turquoise caftan over my head, I grabbed the cloth with the bread and water bag and at the last moment, threw the General's dark cape around me; it would blend into the night. I ran to the back of the tent, opened the flap and crawled through. I was out.

Stars filled the night sky. The moon would rise in less than an hour and turn the rocky hills white. I found one of the trails in the cliff face that ascended more slowly, and began picking my way through the gravel and rocks, as silent as I could be. I hardly dared breathe.

The sounds of the camp, the laughter and talking of men, echoed through the ravine. They might even be joking about the General, making lewd suggestions about the Egyptian witch who pleasured him. Of course, they never imagined in their wildest fantasies that he lay dead in a pool of his own blood.

I clutched the bloody dagger in my right hand. If captured, I had to drive the blade deep into my own throat. My own imagination was not wild enough to describe what the Persians would do to me now.

Chapter 17 Falcon

I stumbled over stones and tripped in small holes, but kept to my feet and kept going. I could not risk hiding; they might find me. My water and food would not last long. I had to keep on the move. But once I climbed over the hill and out of sight of the camp, I wasn't sure which direction to turn.

Desert and wild mountains lay to the east ending at the Red Sea. More desert and mountains lay to the south with miles of wilderness before meeting caravan trails. The Persians had arrived from the north. There could be more Persians; there could be a whole army of Persians. I needed to go west, toward the Nile. But west was the direction they would look for me.

I had to be as far away as possible by daybreak, but had no bearings without the sun. Was I going in circles? Hundreds of trails wound through the rocks and gullies. I didn't know which one to take. I panicked that after hours of trekking, I might end up where I started.

Even with a bright moon, the canopy of stars over my head blazed. I spotted *Meskhetiu*, the Ox Foreleg, pointing the way to the Star of the North. I wondered if Hetmus-hor still lived. I wondered if River God looked up at the stars now and thought of me. River God. It seemed lifetimes since I tasted you on the Nile. I came back through the Red Mirror for you. Where are you now?

Alone. I was so alone. And it was all my own doing. This is no time for your foolishness, River God had told me. And what of my Abydos dream? Hathor had saved me then.

Please, Hathor, do not desert me! I have been foolish, but I have learned. Give me another chance! Please show me the way.

The moon was enormous with intricate etchings of deep shadow; the ridges on the surface reflected back the barren landscape around me.

A black dot, barely visible, appeared in the white glow. I watched it grow larger and larger until I could make out the silhouette of wings. As if gliding on a moonbeam, the falcon drifted toward me.

Hathor's voice was barely a whisper as she flew past my ear.

"Follow me, Isis. Trust me to lead you to your fate."

Perhaps I hallucinated, but I didn't care if the falcon existed in this world or the land of dreams. I would follow wherever she led.

I traveled in the cool of the morning and rested in the shade during the heat of the day. I needed to conserve water. I was sheltering in a small cave high on a rough hillside when I saw the dust of many horsemen far below me and far away. I thought they might be Egyptian, but could as easily be Persian. I resisted shouting and letting the echo carry my voice to them; I dared not risk giving my position away.

The falcon circled overhead. She seemed distant too. I felt alone in the universe. The goatskin water bag was near empty; I had long ago eaten the bread. My feet were cut and bruised; pains shot up my legs with each step.

I could hardly remember the time before my misery. Everywhere I looked, I saw the General's eyes and the bright red of his blood against the green scarf.

Lying back on the rocks, in a tiny shaded crevice, I drifted back to the Nile. It brought me peace to summon the warm, damp air of the river and the sound of the water rushing past.

When I dreamed, two giants lifted me with four hands and lowered me gently onto the East Bank, under the sycamore trees by the hunting lodge. They stroked my breasts and lingered between my loins, taking turns teasing me with their tongues, licking and sucking, each mouth with its own unique rhythm.

The baboons made a great racket and flocks of white herons rose into the sky. It seemed that my life had begun there on the edge of the river, that everything before that morning was just a dream. Before I woke, I saw that the faces of the giants were River God and Hetmus-hor.

I stumbled down a steep incline to a *wadi* that wound through the hills toward the west. The ground was flat and less rocky, easier on my bruised feet and tired legs. The falcon circled overhead in wide arcs.

The sun burned down without mercy. At least there was no dry wind to suck the last of the moisture from my battered body. The heavy cape around my shoulders protected my skin from the sun and kept my perspiration from evaporating. It covered the silk caftan which would have flashed bright turquoise for miles. As much as I wanted to be found, my life depended on it being by the right person.

More in a stupor than awake, I forced my feet to keep moving forward. I was alone in the stillness of the canyon; I saw no other life. The falcon circled in a white sky. I came around a deep bend in the river bed and instantly flattened myself against the cliff.

A group of men rested just ahead; they wore the heavy robes of desert people, no matter the heat. Their heads were wrapped in turbans fashioned of colored cloth, all blue like the sky, except one man whose turban was red.

They took shelter from the heat of the day in the shadows of large boulders and strange-looking brown bushes. They did not talk. The stillness hummed in my ears.

I eased backward slowly until hidden by a sharp turn in the cliff.

My body was glued to the canyon wall. I closed my eyes and took several deep breaths. I couldn't go forward and couldn't go back. Behind me stretched miles of *wadi* leading away from the Nile. The cliffs were too steep to climb out.

They were a ragtag lot, too few for a proper caravan, and caravans don't roam the wild mountains. Traders follow routes that lead from oasis to oasis. They must be hiding, like me.

The guttural sounds of a Semitic tongue carried in the absolute quiet. I caught a few words; the men were from the Island of the Arabs, the land that lies between the Red and Persian Seas.

Beastly sounds joined the men's voices—sounds nothing like the high whinny of a horse or complaining of a donkey. In the brief moment when I glimpsed the men, I hadn't seen any sign of animals.

Inching slowly forward, I stretched just enough to peer around the corner. The brown bushes were not bushes at all, but camels—monstrous beasts with huge humps on their backs, lying with bellies on the ground, their legs folded at the knees and tethered with rope.

A few camels had chair-like saddles on top of their humps, secured by straps tied around the belly. The men climbed into seats and whipped the camels with slender rods. First the back legs extended; the men tipped at a sharp angle toward the ground. Then the front legs straightened, and the men sat perched high in the air.

I panicked. Were they travelling toward me or away? I looked around for tracks and saw a wide trail of disturbed sand in the center of the *wadi*. I'd been too dazed to notice. *Be more alert!*

But the tracks meant we were going in the same direction. I could follow them out of here.

Led by the red turban, the caravan waddled down the riverbed away from me, blue heads swaying as if they rode the swells of the sea.

I waited until they turned the next bend in the *wadi* and then started after them, always hugging the edge of the sheer cliffs.

The shadows grew long; I could no longer see Ra from the bottom of the canyon. The sky was the deeper blue of afternoon, but the air still unbearably hot. The falcon glided in giant circles above my head, not flapping her wings for long periods of time.

Vultures also circled the ravine. Could they smell my hunger and thirst?

One step, then the next, followed by another. If I allowed myself to think of the pain in my feet and legs, I would give up and lie down to die.

The loose stones of a landslide tripped me, and I stumbled. A cobra curled not three feet from my bloodied sandals. He reared his head; only his tail remained curled on the rock. His hood fanned out around his open mouth. The forked tongue flicked in and out between sharp fangs. I didn't move; I didn't blink.

His swaying head mesmerized me; I heard the whistle of the wind as a snake charmer's flute echoing down the *wadi*. Tiny droplets of clear liquid glistened at the tips of his fangs. Tall as me, he stared straight into my eyes.

The slightest flinch, maybe only a blink, and he would strike. The venom of the cobra brings death quickly. It would paralyze my lungs; I would be dead in less than an hour. My breathing was shallow, my chest barely moved. My dry tongue was fat and filled my mouth.

A shadow fell across the rocks. The movement distracted the snake. He turned his head away from me. I leapt to the side, throwing my heavy cape over my head and arms. The cobra should have struck, but the vulture seized his hooded head in its talons and carried the snake high into the sky.

My feet carried me blindly over the rocky sand; I saw only the forked tongue and sharp tips of fangs. When my sandal sank into a hole, I fell into terrible images of eyes: the cobra, the gazelle, and finally the General.

It was dark when I woke. Animals scurried around the rocks, coming out in the cool to feed. I went forward, but not far.

The men gathered around a fire, eating their evening meal. They must have water. My tongue was as swollen as when I dug my way out of the sand at the chariot. My lips were so cracked, I could taste blood when I tried to moisten them. If I didn't get water, I would die. I might not last another day in this heat.

My hand touched the dagger still tied around my waist, under the turquoise silk caftan. Wait until they sleep, then sneak into their camp. It was a wild plan, but I was desperate. I refused to die of thirst in this burned-out ditch.

The fire burned to embers. There was no moon. The Arabs posted no guard. All was quiet except for snoring of men and occasional low grumbles from the animals.

I arranged the heavy cape around me so that my form was as tight and controlled as possible. Edging cautiously along the rock wall, I blended into the shadows. When opposite the dying fire, I stepped away from the side. Impossibly quiet, my feet walked on a cushion of air.

A goatskin water bag lay on the ground close to a camel; I couldn't believe my luck. I lifted the bag an inch at a time. A camel snorted and grumbled and the nearest man stirred. I stood perfectly still, watching him. He rolled over and farted, but didn't wake.

My stomach growled with hunger, but I had to be content with water. One shouldn't tempt fate. I backtracked to the edge of the *wadi*, and then remembered my footprints in the sand. Retracing my steps, I bent from the waist and brushed the edge of my cape against the loose earth, spreading it over the imprint of my sandals.

I would have made it away but for the jackal stepping too close to the edge of the ridge above, starting the rockslide. Pebbles cascaded down, loosening more and more rocks the further they tumbled. A shower of stones fell all around me. Some hit me on the shoulders and back.

The racket of the falling rocks wakened the camels first; they pulled at their tethers, trying to stand, making hellish noises. I suppose the men feared ambush, because they were instantly alert. Starlight flashed off the blades of their knives.

I froze, hoping the General's dark cloak blended into the black contours of the cliff. But they saw me almost at once.

The air exploded in wild shouting, and they rushed me, their knives raised. I threw my hood back so they could see my pale face and thick wig, praying they would recognize an Egyptian woman, even in the light of the stars.

They moved to encircle me, as natural as a wolf pack, no word spoken between them. The man facing me had the yellow eyes of a wolf jackal.

"I am goddess woman!" I shouted at them in the little Arabic I knew.

They were visibly shaken. The tribes of the desert are a superstitious lot. They believe a beautiful witch lives in the mountains and steals men's souls while they sleep. They were frightened of me. I took advantage of it.

"I go home. Big gold."

They relaxed slightly and glanced at each other. They definitely liked the mention of gold.

"Egypt big happy. Give gold very big."

I stepped forward one step and the yellow-eyed man in the red turban stepped back.

"I want water. I want eat."

Summoning just a whisper of the Power, I started toward the embers of the campfire. The yellow-eyed man moved aside and let me pass. My feet felt as large and heavy as those of the camels, but I walked with shoulders back and head high.

I eased to the ground beside the campfire and took a drink from the goatskin bag. Drawn from a desert well, the water was brackish but tasted sweeter than honeyed tea to my parched mouth. I took small sips, giving it time to settle.

They stood around the embers and stared at me; some dared whisper to each other.

"Give me food," I commanded.

Bread appeared, and I ate.

"Tomorrow ride camel."

Wrapping the wool cloak tight around me, I lay down beside the coals and pretended to sleep. So far they seemed awed by me. I wanted to keep it that way. I would show them no fear.

No one came near. They melted away. I could hear hurried whispers. They must have agreed on something, because soon it was silent. Then I heard soft snoring again and allowed myself to sleep

Chapter 18 Rescue

My little caravan of twenty camels wound its way down the *wadi*. Riding atop the hump was much more difficult than it looked, but I would have endured anything to be off my bleeding feet.

The men seemed spooked; I caught them glancing in my direction but never once would they look me in the eye. Their night must have been filled with frightening dreams; they probably still feared I was the witch who would steal their souls.

After midday, the caravan left the bleak mountains and began the long, dusty trek across the desert plateau. The Arabs stopped as usual for the heat of the day, and I napped in the shade of the camel's hump. Before I closed my eyes, I saw the falcon circling overhead.

In the land of the dreams, I visited my temple garden with the song of the nightingale, the sweet scent of gardenia and the moist tongue of River God. But his face kept changing from River God to Hetmus-hor and back again.

A horse approached; I felt the thunder of its hooves vibrating in the hard earth. The rider drew closer and closer; my eyes strained to see in the white sunlight. Waves of heat rose up and distorted the shape. Was it a mirage?

Dust blew into my eyes and blinded me. The pounding of hooves stopped, and I heard the heavy breathing of the winded horse. When I looked again, my slave Goliath was leaping to the ground.

"O Hathor! Thank you! Thank you!"

I rocked back and forth, holding myself.

Goliath rushed to me and then stopped; he had never touched me, not even to brush against me. I went to my knees and grabbed his ankles, my lips on his feet. I would have cried a river, but the desert had sucked the last tear.

I saw nothing but Goliath's feet, as massive to my eyes as those of the God Min in his temple. I tried to stand, but the pain in my feet was so intense, I collapsed. Goliath lifted me into his arms, not allowing himself to look upon my face. He stood like a giant basalt statue of a Nubian pharaoh. My arms were around his neck, my face in his massive chest. I don't know where I got the strength to hold him so tight.

More horses approached and suddenly, as if they rode straight from my dreams, River God and Hetmus-hor thundered up and dismounted together. The two men stood side by side, Hetmus-hor half a head taller than River God. Goliath, holding me in his arms, towered over all. For what seemed like an eternity, no one moved. The shadow of the falcon circled all of us.

"Isis!" Hetmus shouted. "Thank Horus, you are alive!"

He rushed forward, pulled me from Goliath into his own arms and crushed me to his body. My bruised and bleeding feet dangled in the air; I clutched his neck as if I would never let go.

I'm not sure I was really aware of who held me. At that moment, it didn't matter. The nightmare was over. I couldn't control my sobs of relief. My parched body even found tears.

I raised my face, and he kissed me full on the mouth; I forgot my blistered lips and drank in his strength. He had saved me. Hetmus had saved me. I kissed him with the passion of gratitude. Then over his shoulder, through my tears of thanks, I met River God's wounded, angry eyes.

Music and laughter carried in the desert air long before we could see the hunting lodge and the flotilla of pleasure boats moored in the rushes of the Nile. Every noble and priest from Hermopolis must have been on the East Bank to greet us.

Ankh-hor, Hetmus' father, was the first. He stepped into our path, flanked by six slaves in shimmering white kilts and blue-and-yellow striped headdresses. Ankh-hor himself wore so much gold, I was nearly blinded looking at him.

"Welcome home, my son, Savior of Priestesses!" he shouted.

A great roar went up when the crowd saw me seated with Hetmus on his white stallion.

"Hetmus! Hetmus! Hetmus!" they chanted. "Long Life! Long Life! Long Life!"

All around was the smell of meat roasting, but it only made me nauseous. Whole oxen, oryx and even hippopotamus turned on spits. Low wooden tables piled high with breads, cheeses and fruits were arranged in long rows. Judging by the shouts and swaggers, the party had long ago started on the sea of *amphorae* of wine.

After the silence of the desert, the clamor deafened me. I was exhausted. My head pounded.

"No one shall see my Isenkhebe Nefrusobek in such a condition!"

The crowd parted for my mother Sit-hathor and the small army of priests trailing her. She dressed for a temple ritual in the solar disk headdress with twin horns and waving ostrich feathers. She even wore the sacred beaded *menit* around her neck. Four slaves bore a blue-tasseled litter to carry me away.

I looked for River God.

He was still mounted on his black stallion with its long mane and tail braided with silver twine. His men gathered around him; sunlight flashed on the metal studs of the round crocodile shields slung across their backs. Shaking their spears and waving short killing swords in circles above their heads, they sang their Commander's praises, competing with the chants for Hetmus-hor.

River God glared at me over the heads of the crowd as if it

were my fault that Hetmus held me, that it was my fault that the crowd praised Hetmus-hor for single-handedly rescuing me. Why had River God not acted first? I could be in his arms now.

He had not spoken to me during the trek back to the Nile, but rode silently in front, leading the way, never looking back at Hetmus and me on the white horse.

When I had asked why River God was not traveling with the Crown Prince to Saïs, his captain told me that as soon as the Commander received word that I'd been lost in the desert, he had commissioned the fastest boat in Khent-min and drove the crew to row round the clock to reach Hermopolis. His cavalry had joined him on the banks of the hunting lodge and spent days in the desert searching with Hetmus-hor until the falcon led them to me.

Waiting inside the splendid tent Sit-hathor had set up for my arrival was Qeb-ha. I kissed his hand and begged his forgiveness. How could I ever have disdained him for being a eunuch? How could I have been so foolish not to see his true worth? *On the road one finds a companion*, he had said to me in Abydos. *In battle one finds a brother—or sister*. But I had wanted neither from him.

"I am only a priest," he said kindly. "The Gods know the impious and the pious man by his heart. The Goddess has judged Isenkhebe to be pious. Why else would Hathor appear as a falcon to lead Isenkhebe out of the desert to us?"

The heat, the thirst, the pain, the fear, the desolation, the panic— everything crashed on me at once. I'd never known such exhaustion.

I lay on the bed and wept for what seemed like hours. My mother held me and would not let anyone near. Maia brought herbed water to soak my swollen and cut feet, but my mother took the bowl and cleaned me herself. The great Sit-hathor shaved my head tenderly with a new copper razor.

"Burn this foul wig," she commanded. "And burn this wretched cape and these sandals as well."

But she fingered the smooth silk of my turquoise caftan in the same way the women in the camp had touched my fine linen hunting gown.

"Keep this. Clean it. But get it out of the tent now! I want nothing of those Persian beasts near my Isenkhebe."

She shaved me and bathed me and massaged the best fragrant oils into my chapped skin. A gown of the finest weave in all Egypt was pulled down over my shoulders, tender and raw from coarse wool chaffing against sunburned skin blasted by sand.

The party outside was loud with singing and the sudden shouts of gamblers. I wondered if River God were still here. He hadn't tried to see me. Hetmus-hor had come to the tent but been turned away. Sit-hathor let him know that she held him responsible for the desert, for the Persians. She gave orders to the priests that no member of Ankh-hor's family be allowed near me.

She didn't ask me anything about what had happened in the camp. No one had asked me. They didn't want to know.

Bathed, oiled and dressed, a glorious new wig on my head and my eyes painted with mica and *kohl*, I lay on the low bed unable to see anything but the shock on the General's face. My lips were too cracked to stain red with pomegranate juice. It was painful to speak, but I did.

"Mother, I must tell you."

"Yes, my beautiful Isis, you must tell all, but later. Forget the desert and be joyful you are safe with us. Hold only happy thoughts in your head and beautiful visions before your eyes."

"But I have visions that won't go away. They are before my eyes when open, and they are there when my lids close."

She sighed and waved everyone away. Her face was sad. I saw a trace of dread in her eyes.

"Then speak, my beauty. Speak of the horrors if you must. But wounds must not be picked too soon. They need time to heal. And remember that this evil happened to your body, not to your soul."

"Mother, my wounds *are* to my soul."

Her eyes widened ever so slightly. She took my hand in hers. Our twin Hathor rings flashed in the light.

"Then we shall call upon the Goddess," she crooned in her voice of liquid gold. "Hathor delivered you from the desert; She shall deliver you from this. But once the words are spoken, purge them from your mind. Those memories will no longer be part of your life."

As she spoke, the Hathor energy flowed through me. I felt the General again—the pain and the ecstasy—and then finally the ride on a comet. I shuddered and exhaled all the air in my lungs; my breath rattled my chest and vibrated in my throat. To my ears the sound was a wail.

"I killed the General, Mother," I whispered. "I made love to him, and then I cut his throat."

Her black eyes opened wide in horror before her lids nearly closed, and she exhaled a long hiss, not unlike that of a cobra.

"He bled to death, Mother. I watched his *Ka* leave his body."

My voice took on a flat quality devoid of emotion. I heard myself speak, yet was detached from the meaning of the words.

"His blood spilled down his chest and onto my hands. It was everywhere. I tried to staunch the bleeding with a green silk scarf."

"Listen to me!" she commanded. "Do not *ever* again speak of love with this animal. You owe him nothing, do you hear? Nothing."

"He had to die, Mother," I sobbed, "but I did not want him to. Can you understand? I did not *want* him to die!"

Sit-hathor leaned forward until I saw nothing but her face. I'd never seen her eyes so glittery, like black glass. Her fingers dug into my shoulders.

"Stop, Isenkhebe! I forbid you to have feelings for that monster!"

I closed my eyes and saw his lifeless eyes. I felt dead myself.

"I had no choice." I said flatly. "It was him or me." At last I was resigned to what was and couldn't be changed.

She relaxed her fingers and kissed me lightly on the forehead.

When she spoke again, her voice was matter-of-fact, as if she commented on a household chore.

"Of course you killed him, my daughter. And I hope you cut off his filthy balls and stuffed them in his vile mouth."

Chapter 19   The Fortune-teller

I heard the pounding of hammer on stone, never ceasing. They must be carving a column just outside my bedchamber.

My ears rang. I felt drugged and disoriented. A door opened; I heard voices. Then Barb rushed in. The property manager followed with a ring of keys in his hand.

"Are you okay?" she asked, her voice filled with alarm. "Do you need a doctor? Should we call 911?"

The manager had his cell phone out, ready to hit send.

"No! Don't call! I'm fine. I was just…sleeping. I didn't hear you knock."

"Sleeping? What is wrong with you?" Barb collapsed on the floor beside me and took my hand. "I've been calling you for *two* days. Your office has been calling you. Why haven't you answered your cell? We thought you'd been kidnapped—or were dead."

I looked at her and wondered how she knew.

"I'd like some water. Would you bring me a glass of water, please?"

The manager walked into the kitchen and opened a cupboard.

I whispered urgently to Barb, "Get him out of here and I'll tell you everything."

"Thank you." I emptied the glass in one go.

The manager studied me for a moment and then asked, "Do you

mind if I have a look around? Make sure everything is okay?"

He didn't wait for my answer but tested the sliding glass doors. They were locked. He stepped into my bedroom. I heard him check the glass doors to the terrace and then go into the walk-in closet and my bathroom. Finally, he checked the second bedroom and bath, and then came back and stood looking down at me.

I still sat on the floor, the empty glass in my hand.

"Everything seems fine." His tone said he didn't believe it. "If you're sure you're okay, then I'll get back to my office. I'll have to file a report though."

"I'm okay. Really I am. Thank you so much for your help. I'm so sorry to be such a...bother." I tried to sound cheerful and normal so he'd leave.

When he finally closed the door behind him, I got up off the floor and headed straight for the toilet. Barb followed me to the door.

"What the hell is going on?" Barb sounded just like my mother when I was in junior high, and she caught a boy in my room.

"Remember I told you about the Red Mirror?"

When I finished, Barb sat motionless and silent on the red modern sofa she hated because she said it hurt her back. Her wheat-colored Dutch boy hair gleamed in the light. She clutched a polka dot throw pillow in her long, thin arms. I had a brief doubt that she had heard me at all. I had doubts that she actually sat there.

Barb looked over at the Red Mirror and then back at me.

"You know," she said quietly, "if I hadn't seen you and Rasheed— *River God*, you say—at the Stirling Club and the connection between you—right from the first moment—I'd think you were out of your mind."

Barb believed me! I never expected anyone to believe me. I could hardly believe myself.

I checked my missed calls. Carla had called yesterday, twice. She answered right away.

"I'm having a party!" She sounded excited; her voice was happy. "I want you to meet my new boyfriend. He's a doll. I'm in love."

Carla fell in love easily and out again just as fast. Beautiful and rich, she had the kind of money you work for, not a trust fund, not easy. She owned a penthouse with a heart-stopping view of the Strip. At the top of her game, she was mature enough to be taken seriously, but young enough to have muscle tone.

Jewish, with shiny black hair cut short like a pixy, she had grown up in Rio and spoke English with the same rapid fire speed as Portuguese. Her mind, too, moved at the speed of light.

I wished I could be more like her. Carla always knew exactly what she wanted and got it. She was spoiled, but she spoiled herself.

"Tonight, darling. Come by after nine. It's intimate, just a few friends."

I knew what that meant. Carla had a lot of friends.

"May I bring someone?"

"Of course! Is he good-looking?"

I laughed. I always laughed a lot with Carla. One of her parties was just what I needed to calm my nerves.

"It's my friend Barb. I promised to see her tonight."

"Of course, bring her along. It's dressy; be sure and tell her that."

She didn't need to remind me. I don't think Carla ever threw a casual party.

On an impulse, I called Elaine. We'd been roommates in college and friends ever since. She was married with two kids and lived in a wonderful two-story colonial on the edge of Amish country.

"Elaine, you believe in reincarnation, don't you? That you've lived other lives?"

"Well, yes, I have my own ideas."

Her voice was calm; Elaine always seemed so tranquil. She reminded me of the nurturing side of Hathor, the benevolent aspects of motherhood and fecundity.

"Do you believe we meet the same people in different lifetimes?"

"I think we encounter the same souls over and over until we learn the lessons we need to teach each other."

"Have we known each before, Elaine?"

"Absolutely. We have known each other before, and we will know each other again."

Rasheed said exactly the same thing the morning he left me in the Wynn.

"You haven't told me why you're asking me all this. What's happened?"

"I'm just sorting some things out. I'll tell you all about it someday, but there's too much to explain right now."

"I'll take the time, if you need me," she offered in the soft, no pressure tone of a good friend.

"No, that's okay. I think I'm starting to understand. Thank you. Thank you so much, Elaine. Say hi to Steve and the kids."

It took a long time to decide what to wear to Carla's party. I dug out a snug, low-cut white top and a long white clingy skirt. At the bottom of my closet, I found gold sandals with turquoise-looking stones embedded across the straps. My feet looked so bare. No henna patterns. I'd seen lots of girls with tiny tattoos on their toes and ankles and always thought it silly. I wasn't so sure anymore.

When I looked into the Red Mirror, I saw Isis in my face. I wet my hair, parted it down the middle and took out the scissors and cut bangs straight across my forehead. It surprised me how much I looked like Isis then. Isis in her wig, of course.

I fastened a heavy gold chain low on my hips and then remembered a necklace my aunt had brought back from one of her trips to Israel. Three golden chains fell across my collar bone with strings of turquoise beads in between. Not quite Egyptian, but close enough.

The valet whisked my car away, and the doorman opened the glass doors into the white marble foyer. Barb was waiting for me in the sleek, ultra-modern lobby dotted with lush orchid bouquets in

Chinese vases.

Barb looked hard at me but didn't say a word until we got into the stainless steel elevator.

"Well, you are certainly playing the part. Did you cut your bangs?"

It was a silly question, and she knew it.

"You look great, Barb."

She did, too. Her flaxen hair glistened. She wore hot pink and yellow. I wondered when we had known each other before.

When we rang the bell, a slim young woman in a black dress, white apron and giant, hoop earrings greeted us and took our coats. Barb followed me down the parquet hallway into the living room with modern paintings in primary colors. A broad terrace furnished with white outdoor sofas and heat lamps stretched outside the open glass doors. The lights of the Strip blazed in the background.

Brazilian jazz played through hidden speakers. Two cooks were busy at the gleaming Viking range; the aroma of *empanadas* wafted through the air. The kitchen was crowded with handsome men in black suits and T-shirts, their hair short and spiky. Most of them were speaking Portuguese.

This was Carla's group of Brazilian friends. Their dates, gorgeous young girls in the shortest of skirts, balanced on the highest of heels. You had to be beautiful to attend Carla's parties—or rich.

A bartender in a white jacket served drinks. Barb and I took flutes with champagne and wandered out onto the terrace, looking for Carla. I spotted her at the edge of the balcony, talking to a small group. Her black pixy hair barely reached the shoulder of the man she leaned into. We maneuvered our way through the sofas, and I eased up beside her.

"Oh my god!" she gushed. "I didn't even know it was you! You look just like Cleopatra!"

She kissed me on both cheeks and beamed. She was positively radiant. Yes, Carla was in love.

"Meet Hector," she said triumphantly. Her black eyes glowed.

"*Encantada*," he said with a wide smile of brilliant white teeth.

I took his hand and smiled back.

"Hello, Hector."

He held onto my hand just a little too long. Carla looked from my face up to his and back again.

"Do you two know each other?"

Hector remained cool, very smooth, but his smile was full of secrets.

"*Si*, but from a very long time ago."

He had the natural confidence that comes with being tall, handsome, and privileged. What had Carla said about him? Something about Argentina and polo?

Barb had a look on her face that shouted, "Oh no, not again!"

I pulled my hand away.

"Carla, this is my friend, Barb. Barb, this is Hector, Carla's boyfriend."

Carla liked the boyfriend bit. She put her arm through Hector's and snuggled against his biceps. Whatever had gone on before, he was hers now.

"Now tell me how you know each other. No secrets allowed!"

Hector smiled at me a little too warmly.

"It was long ago, Carlita, in another life." He kissed her lightly on the cheek and said, "Please excuse me while I get another cerveza. *Más champaña*, Ladies?"

With another gracious smile and slight bow of his head, he excused himself, "*Con permiso.*"

I don't think anyone noticed his sideways glance into my eyes as he squeezed by me, his dinner jacket brushing my arm. Carla's starry eyes followed him.

"Isn't he gorgeous? He's a perfect gentleman, but not too much, if you know what I mean?"

Her eyes twinkled, and her dimples deepened. I knew just what she meant.

A handsome couple joined us. They knew Barb and started to talk real estate. I slipped away.

The hallway to Carla's bedroom was empty. The door to her bathroom opened with a blaze of bright light. A man with white hair and a tuxedo came out and smiled.

"It's all yours," he said gallantly.

Hector waited by the picture window in Carla's bedroom, leaning against the frame. The Stratosphere looked close enough to reach out and touch.

"Hello, Isis."

I walked right up to him, put my hands on his chest and leaned my head back. He was so tall.

"Hello, Hetmus."

Hector took me by the shoulders and pulled me tight to him, my hands still on his chest, my elbows crushed between us. He was like a man who had thirsted on the desert for days. He wrapped his long arms around me, nearly lifting me off my feet, kissing my lips, my neck, my shoulders, my throat, everywhere he could find flesh. His breath was hot and moist on my skin. An image of him devouring me flashed in my mind; he could have swallowed me whole.

I slipped my arms under his dinner jacket and pulled myself into him, burying my face in his broad chest. I smelled starch and the faintest scent of soap. He was rock hard and huge against my waist. I leaned further into him and swayed back and forth, feeling his hardness roll on my belly.

With no effort at all, he lifted me into his arms, my feet dangling down, just as he had held me in the desert under the shadow of the circling falcon.

"I've waited a few thousand years for this," he breathed in my ear as he carried me to Carla's bed.

There among the silk pillows and pile of fur coats, he lay beside me and ran his long fingers down the length of my body from my face to my ankles, his eyes soaking up my every curve. The heat of his hands warmed me. He stroked me all over; I stretched and purred.

"You are perfect, Isis. I could never tire of touching you."

The bulge between his impossibly long legs grew larger. I slid down the zipper and slipped my fingers first inside the light wool and then through the gap in the soft cotton of his briefs. He throbbed hot and thick in my hand as I milked him.

My fingers swirled on the smooth wet skin of his engorged knob. When I pulled the skin back down his shaft, the knob popped larger and swelled more.

I nibbled him and sucked him and licked the small glistening drops.

Another man might have lain back and let me pleasure him, but not Hector. All the while I fondled him, his hands roamed my body, exploring my every curve.

"Let me pleasure you," he whispered.

Then his long fingers went deep into my canal and straight to a place no other man had ever found. The spot that I'd heard of but believed was a myth. The G-Spot. It existed, alright. O Hathor! Does it ever exist.

Time stopped. I forgot Hector's swollen shaft. I forgot the party outside. I forgot everything except the feel of his fingers rotating on that magic spot. Burning heat radiated deep into my buttocks and loins. My knees relaxed outward. I was spread wide. I floated on the velvet sea with sensuous, rolling, undulating waves crashing on my shore, one after another washing over me, drowning me in pleasure.

I never wanted it to end. I wanted never to move. I wanted Hector's finger on that spot forever.

I would never have left Carla's bed if not for Barb.

She appeared in the doorway with her lips pursed like an angry schoolmarm. All that was missing was her hands on her hips. Waves of rage filled the room.

"I, uh, hate to break this up, but Carla is looking for you, Hector."

She spoke to Hector, but glared at me, her eyes shooting daggers.

What are you doing? Have you lost your mind?

"Go to her," I told him.

Thank Hathor, it was Barb who had come in and not Carla. There was no telling what Brazilian Carla might have done. What would I do if I found my boyfriend fingerfucking one of my friends in my bed?

"I am not giving you up," Hector said as he straightened his clothes. "I will do whatever it takes to have you—*cualquier cosa.*"

When he disappeared through the doorway, Barb looked at me with disgust.

"God, could you be more obvious? Both of you disappearing like that? And in Carla's *bed*?"

"I need a drink." It was the only answer I had for her.

I ordered single malt, straight with a splash, no ice. The bartender filled my short glass three quarters full. He knew the code of those words. My hands trembled.

Barb glared at me. I could read her thoughts. *Get yourself under control, girl.*

I thought she might lecture me right there at the bar, but a lush, busty redhead in a tight blue knit sheath squeezed through the crowded kitchen to order a glass of Chardonnay.

"Have you seen the fortune-teller yet?" she asked. "He'll blow your mind."

Barb went in first. I admit to being a little scared. My mind still dwelled in the past, the distant past; I didn't know if I could handle the future. When she came out, it was with a dazed expression.

"It's really, *really* strange. He told me things that nobody could possibly know."

I didn't think Barb had any secrets.

"Were they good things?" I couldn't bear any doom and gloom. I was far too emotionally fragile for anything but good news.

The fortune-teller sat in a darkened room at a small table. A low lamp burned nearby with a red shade. He didn't look directly at me, but motioned for me to sit in the straight-backed chair on the opposite side of the table. The bare surface of the wooden top gleamed.

His suit was all wrong; it didn't fit him at all. Even his body language was awkward. The way he moved and the way he spoke made me think he wasn't all there, not crazy or retarded, but autistic maybe.

Taking my hands in his, he closed his eyes. His body swayed from side to side. He mumbled. I couldn't make out anything he said. Should I ask him to speak up? Then he stopped rocking with a jerk, and sucked in a short breath. His hot and sweaty hands gripped my cold fingers in an iron vise.

"You are in great danger," he intoned.

His voice came from some distant place, the sound hollow, like a soft echo. I had the sense he wasn't here in this room, but far away.

"You think you are safe. Everyone thinks you are safe. But they are wrong."

I hated this. I didn't like it all. This wasn't what you'd expect at a party. He should be telling me that I would meet a tall, dark stranger and that I didn't need to worry about money.

"You have to get out. To stay is more horrible than you can imagine. They will do terrible things to you, if they find you. They will find you, if you stay."

I pulled my hands away. I wanted to put them over my ears so I couldn't hear more.

"You have to go back, Isis. You have to go back, or you will suffer. You can't imagine the suffering."

I stood up so abruptly, the chair tipped over and hit the parquet floor with a smack.

"Go back, Isis," he urged. "Go back and save yourself."

My heart exploded in my chest. I couldn't get out of the room fast enough. I fled through the door and leaned against the wall in the hallway, bending from the waist, gulping air.

Barb, completely freaked, held me tight. "My god, what did he say to you? It's just a party game. Nothing he says is real."

She had forgotten her own awe when she exited the room. People looked at me, trying to decide if I had drunk too much or overdosed. I heard "911" for the second time today.

I imagined how ridiculous I looked, dressed up like Halloween. Barb maneuvered me into the third bedroom and closed the door behind us.

"Sit down," she commanded. "Put your head between your knees. Don't move. I'm getting you some water. "

I was dizzy and felt sick and hoped I wouldn't vomit on Carla's Marimekko rug.

Voices conferred outside the door, but no one came in. Barb reappeared with a glass of water and made me take sips. Then Carla was there.

"What happened? Did you drink too much? Why don't you lie down? You can sleep here tonight. Don't worry about driving home." She was distraught and caring at the same time.

I had a hard time understanding; voices sounded thick and syrupy, as if played too slow on a tape recorder.

Barb was so apprehensive, I could almost see her wring her hands. Hector stood behind her, distress all over his face. He came forward and bent on his knee. He took my hands in his and leaned so close that only inches separated us.

"I am here for you," he whispered softly. "Whatever it is, I am here."

I pulled myself together. Isis wouldn't sit paralyzed on the edge of a bed.

"I think I'm fine now. In fact, I know I'm fine." My voice sounded strong; I almost convinced myself. "I feel like an idiot. I can't believe I caused such a scene. I hope you'll forgive me, Carla."

Hector appeared with my coat and bag and announced he was driving me home. At first Carla looked at him in bewilderment, then stared hard at him and then me.

Once the excitement was over, everyone else went back to the bar. There was no sign of the fortune-teller.

Rage and jealousy seethed in Carla's eyes when the elevator doors slid shut. Well, there goes that friend. I really didn't think it was my fault. Blame Isis. Blame Isis for everything.

Blame Isis for my going back.

When Hector opened the door to my condo, Aisha was there immediately, rubbing against his legs. He picked her up, stroking her black fur. She didn't struggle at all, but relaxed into his arms and purred louder.

"Please don't say anything to Carla," I pleaded. "Not yet. It's too soon."

"It's not too soon for me, Isis."

He wrapped me in his arms, but this time he held me without crushing. His lips lingered on mine, his tongue gentle, penetrating, but not devouring. He didn't stroke me; he didn't explore me. He didn't use his hands at all except to hold me.

But I felt his need all through his body. My body responded with a will of its own. The heat of a sudden flush warmed my skin. I pressed into him and felt him rock-hard again. I wanted so badly to touch his hardness, to fondle and stroke him, to make him grow larger still, but I didn't. I wanted to please him and for him to please me. But not now.

"Hector, I'm not ready."

He was gentleman enough to stop, but I could see he was confused and frustrated. And why wouldn't he be?

"It's too soon," I said lamely.

He took my face in his hands and raised my chin so I looked straight into his eyes. The little red specks sparkled in the brown.

"It could never be too soon for us, Isis."

He stroked the side of my cheek, then stroked once across my forehead as if to wipe the tension away.

"Put every worry out of your mind. Nothing will happen to you when you are with me."

He kissed me again, very lightly, just a brush on the lips, and then whispered in my ear, *"Hasta mañana."*

He closed the door and I went straight to my laptop and googled Cambyses. It's all just history now. The Persians routed the Egyptians, and Psamtik the new Pharaoh lost everything, almost 2500 years of Egypt, to the Persians.

It hit me hard when I read it. I shuddered to think of Maia, Qeb-ha, Hetmus-hor—and River God. What had been their fates?

What had been *my* fate?

Everyone thinks you are safe. But they are wrong.

If I didn't get Isis out of Egypt, the Persians would get me in the end.

Go back, Isis. Go back and save yourself.

PART THREE

The Great Green

Chapter 20 Hermes Trismegistus

It was unbearably hot. Heavy moist air pressed on my flesh. I reclined near-naked on my sofa, sipping watered wine, watching flowering trees and full-naked farmers slide past. Stands of papyrus choked the river banks. No cliffs here and no golden sand creeping up to the water's edge. The lush fields of the Delta flowed into the horizon.

Miles to the south, just past the ancient pyramids of Giza, the Nile had divided into seven smaller branches all streaming to the Great Green. River traffic here was heavy; the Nile was jammed with vessels of all sizes and shapes. With little space to row, our oarsmen relaxed against the wooden benches, joking and singing bawdy songs.

Then without warning, papyrus factories replaced green fields, and we suddenly arrived at the river port of Saïs. Metal clanged against wood and stone; the clamor of voices in dozens of languages rang in my ears. Boats large and small jockeyed for positions at the jammed riverfront lined with carved painted columns holding a stone roof.

The marketplace that sheltered in the arcade's deep shade spilled over into white sunlight. Obelisks with gold tips gleamed, and brightly painted temples sparkled like jewels—sapphire, emerald, ruby and citrine.

Our oarsmen tossed thick ropes of braided sedge to dockworkers drenched in sweat; their muscles rippled across their broad shoulders. Their black skin glistened.

My Nubian slave Goliath waited near the carved bowsprit of bundled papyrus reeds, ready to be the first ashore. Standing close by him was Qeb-ha.

The old priest and I exchanged nods. His amethyst earring swung gently back and forth. I read relief on his face; his eyes smiled. Saïs, at last.

It is on the road that one finds a companion. It is in battle that one finds a brother.

A party of priests in long white skirts accompanied by armed temple guards in short kilts and blue triangular headdresses arrived to escort us to the Temple of Neith.

Thank Hathor, we wouldn't spend our days on this crowded barge in the noisy harbor. I sensed no imminent danger. We heard no buzz of Persians or war. I had time. Isis still had time.

We passed through massive wooden gates from the madness of the street to the serenity of the temple parkland. At the heart of the garden lay a sacred lake reflecting the thick foliated columns of the main temple building.

Clumps of hollyhocks, lilies and delphiniums bloomed among slim obelisks and fat sphinxes. White, blue and pink lotus floated on dozens of still ponds. Peacocks with spread tails roamed the grounds; iridescent dragonflies swarmed in the rushes.

Armed with long spears and rectangular shields as tall as their torsos, six Temple Guards in blue headdresses stood at attention by the gate. The heavy cedar doors clanged shut behind us. Only the invited may enter this world; I prayed to the Goddess Neith that Her walls would keep me safe.

Sometime in the night, warm hands moved across my breasts and over my belly, caressing my hips and the slope of my thighs. Fingers climbed my mound and descended into the wetness. They lingered until my bud swelled and then moist lips explored all of me, leaving no place unkissed.

Soft music drifted from a hidden spot under the arbors. A gentle breeze moved the palm fronds. There was a faint scent of myrrh. I moaned in my sleep; Pehtes purred in my ear.

"Isis," a low voice breathed my private name, but I wasn't sure who. "Isis. Isis."

I didn't open my eyes. I wanted it to go on; I didn't want it to be a dream.

Bright morning sunshine flooded the balcony when Maia came with breakfast of fruit and *seremt*, a wheat porridge liquid enough to drink. I had no priestess duties in this temple; I took my time on the marble terrace overlooking a pond surrounded by sunny chrysanthemums and fiery celosia. The Nile, noisy and crammed with boats, lay in the distance.

Maia dressed me in a long white linen gown of tiny pleats with broad straps covering my breasts. Silver serpents with emerald eyes coiled around my bare upper arms and encircled my slender ankles. Matching silver serpents dangled from my earlobes.

She was finishing the final adjustments to my short wig trimmed with silver tassels when the message came. The small scroll of plain papyrus with Greek letters said only that I should go with the guard. The blood drained from Maia's face.

"Do you know anything about this?" I asked.

She only shook her head. Fear flashed in her eyes.

A lone Temple Guard waited in the reception room. He carried a spear but no shield; a short iron thrusting sword hung in his belt. He stood fearfully straight and didn't look at me. Goliath glared at the guard and kept his hand on his own sword.

"Fetch me the heart amulet, Maia. The one my mother Sithathor gave me in the Temple."

I followed the guard, and Goliath followed me. We passed through two open courtyards with porticos of papyriform columns covered in grape vines before entering a green granite chapel. The guard turned in the first vestibule and went along a deserted corridor ending in tall double doors. He knocked. We waited only a few moments.

A priest with shaven head, long white linen kilt, and bare chest with a broad golden collar opened the door, but didn't speak; a leopard skin cloaked his stooped shoulders. His right hand held a torch. He was old, older than Qeb-ha. I wondered if he also was a eunuch. He smiled to reassure me.

Half of his teeth were missing; the remaining were dark as aged ivory. Enormous gold ankhs stretched his earlobes and grazed his shoulders at the bottom of a stubby neck. He motioned for me to follow.

The guard stepped aside; he wasn't going any further. When Goliath moved to follow me, the guard held the spear in his path and shook his head.

"Only the priesthood may pass through these doors. All others are forbidden to enter."

"He goes everywhere with me," I protested.

"The penalty for entering is death."

The guard looked straight at me for the first time. He didn't move the spear.

The priest said nothing.

I nodded to Goliath, and he reluctantly stayed behind as the priest closed the heavy wooden door and bolted it from the inside.

We entered shadow and total silence. The narrow hallway with vaulted ceilings had no windows or doors. Our footsteps in leather sandals echoed in the stillness. I had the feeling eons passed between visits here.

The passage widened into a small chapel area with a false door carved into the end wall. Torches flamed in niches on both sides. Through this illusory stone door passed the *Ka* spirit to visit from the afterlife.

The priest bent to the floor; his fingers went straight to an unseen lever on the bottom of the carved door jamb. Stone ground on stone and a draft of cool air blew across my cheek. The torches sputtered for a moment, then burned straight again.

I stepped closer, lighting the shadows to make out a narrow gap in the corner just wide enough for a person to squeeze through.

The priest took the torch from me and disappeared through the opening. I followed, and he quickly shoved the stone portal closed after me.

Travertine stairs disappeared into black. I counted thirty steps as we went down; we were deep in the earth beneath the temple. Our single torch lit a small circle around us.

The stairway cut through a domed ceiling painted midnight blue with exotic white symbols glowing amid hundreds of yellow stars. I couldn't remember ever having seen the glyphs before. I certainly couldn't read what they said.

The steps ended in a perfectly round room, walls painted the same deep blue as the dome. Ebony doors etched with more of the alien glyphs, this time in gold and silver, encircled us.

The priest inserted a heavy ankh-shaped key hanging from a golden cord into the lock of a door with a seven-pointed star above the lintel. A tunnel led to a black hole, and I followed him into the void.

The flame of our fire burned in utter darkness. How I wished I also had a torch. Moisture seeped through the sandstone walls and ceiling; the stink of mildew filled my nose. The only sounds were our footsteps on stone and the hissing of the torch. The tunnel turned and twisted until the priest finally stopped at a single wooden door. That door, too, opened with the ankh key, and our torch lit a spiral staircase twisting into the bowels of the earth.

The steps were steep with no railing. He moved quickly for an old man; his feet knew the way. I followed him cautiously, never taking my hand from the slimy stone walls, careful not to slip and tumble to the bottom. There was darkness above and blackness below.

A triangular red door with a seven-pointed silver star at the apex waited for us at the bottom of the stairwell. The priest knocked hard and then soft. The door opened wide; I closed my eyes against a light as bright as the noon sun when exiting a temple.

A hand took my hand and led me inside, and the red door shut firmly behind me. I was deep in the earth and at the end of a maze. I resisted the wave of claustrophobia that washed over me. I resisted the feeling of being entombed.

Dozens of lanterns hung from stone arches. Thousands of scrolls filled niches in the walls. I had a vision of catacombs lined with bodies bundled in white. If interred here alive, the reading on these shelves might fill the days of a long life.

A tall man with long silvery hair stood beside a square wooden table covered with rolled and unrolled papyri. Seven-pointed stars, embroidered in silvery threads, shimmered in his blue robe. He was the Wizard from my Abydos dream. He had nothing in his hands though—no tablet and no sword; he reached out both hands to me. His eyes were pale, almost without color; I didn't think it possible for him ever to go in the sun.

"I am Hermes Trismegistus," he said in lilting Greek. "Welcome my daughter, Isenkhebe Nefrusobek, to the Library of Neith, the greatest Mystery School of all time."

My father's palms were large and square with almost no lines. Sit-hathor's gold heart amulet glinted against the smooth skin. Some say you can see a person's character and destiny in the lines and shape of their hands. Hermes had only three lines in his palm; his path must be exceedingly clear.

He gazed at the heart amulet; the ghosts of fond memories passed liked wispy clouds across his face. After a few moments in the pleasures of the past, he returned to me.

"I did not need the amulet to know you, my daughter. The beauty and strength of your mother is reflected clearly in your face."

Hermes Thrice-Greatest was a warm man who smiled easily. He

put me at ease with idle talk about Sit-hathor and Thebes while he moved aside the scrolls, replacing them with three silver chalices filled with wine. He squeezed my hand in a loving way before passing me a chalice rimmed with stars and crescent moons.

"I hear you also have a sharp wit. I admire a woman with intelligence as much as I admire a woman with beauty. You, my dear, are blessed with both."

He turned his head and spoke into the shadows. "Do you not agree, Antinous? Is my daughter not both beautiful and quick?"

I was thrown a bit off balance that Hermes hadn't told me that we weren't alone.

"Your daughter is indeed beautiful, Hermes."

Antinous had the voice of an educated Greek, deep, musical, trained for oratory and theatre. He didn't seem ready to concede my wit.

I should have noticed it odd that Hermes set three chalices on the table. I felt at a disadvantage, as if I had been scrutinized and judged and failed the first test.

The Greek leaned casually against a wall, muscular arms lightly crossed. A blue *chiton*, belted at the waist, ended halfway up his wrestler thighs; fabric draped in soft folds from his broad left shoulder across his muscled chest. The right shoulder was bare, as were his magnificent biceps and perfect forearms. The contour of his muscles ended in strong wrists and graceful hands.

His beauty was so perfect, he might have been sculpted from marble. A Greek statue, but clothed.

A mane of waves with streaks of gold crowned his head; ringlets fell on his brow and around his ears. He had hair you wanted to run your fingers through and watch the curls spring back. He had a body you wanted to run your fingers over and watch the gooseflesh rise.

Antinous took the third chair at the table. He was even more beautiful up close. His pale skin was flawless. I didn't think it possible for eyes to be so blue. He was reserved and just a little cool—very hard to read.

Once Antinous joined us, Hermes grew more solemn. I sensed he was ready to move on to the purpose of our meeting.

"All knowledge is contained in these scrolls, including many secrets." He swept his arm in an arc to point out the hundreds of papyri neatly stacked in the niches.

"Secrets?" I asked. "Is that why I am here?"

"I have heard you are both impatient and direct," Hermes chuckled. But he smiled the indulgent smile of a doting father.

Antinous watched me a little too intently; he made me mildly uneasy. Hermes appeared not to be in a hurry to divulge why he had sent for me. He settled back in his chair and took a sip of wine before continuing.

"So, Isenkhebe, what have your tutors taught you about Atlantis?"

"Atlantis?" I don't know what I had expected, but it wasn't that he would start out with a fable.

"Atlantis is...well...a mythical land that supposedly sank into the sea?" I answered uncertainly, my voice going up at the end with a question. What other answer could there possibly be?

"Let me assure you that Atlantis was, in fact, very real."

I glanced quickly at Antinous. Both Hermes and Antinous watched me, Hermes with a bit of amusement in his eyes, Antinous quite serious. They seemed to be waiting for me say something. Another test?

"You have called me here for a reason, my father. I assume it has something to do with Atlantis. Am I to guess, or will you tell me?"

"A sharp tongue like your mother!" Hermes laughed out loud and poured himself more wine.

Antinous didn't laugh. In fact, his eyes narrowed just a bit, and a rather deep crease appeared between his eyebrows.

Hermes studied me for a moment. I had the impression he was taking me step-by-step to judge if I were worthy.

"Atlantis was a very advanced culture many thousands of years ago."

Hermes' voice took on a dreamlike quality, a bit like when he first saw the amulet and was transported back to a time when he and my mother were young. At any rate, he seemed far away, seeing things that only he could see.

"Much more advanced than ours. Yet in some ways, very much the same."

A moment or two passed in silence. The lamps burned evenly. The air was still as death this deep in the earth. I wondered if I were expected to respond, to ask how they were more advanced, or how we were the same.

But then Hermes came back. His voice was brisk, and he looked directly at me.

"They understood that the physical world is a reflection of the spiritual world. The world below and the world above mirror each other. We Greeks call it *microcosm* and *macrocosm*."

He stopped to give me a moment to consider what he was saying.

"The Cosmic Code. Form comes from thought. One form of matter can be changed to another," he went on.

Images of medieval alchemists turning lead into gold flashed through my mind.

"But like us, the Atlanteans were greedy and arrogant. They experimented and played with natural forces, breeding monsters that were part man-part beast. But the end came when they released a cosmic energy they could not control. It ripped their world apart in a runaway chain reaction."

"Were there any survivors?" I envisioned a massive nuclear catastrophe, one large enough to destroy a whole world.

"A very few. Some came to the Delta ages ago. The simple men living here made their man-beast abominations into gods."

Cow-eared Hathor. Ibis-headed Thoth.

A dozen more beast-gods ran through my head, but I asked, "Are the strange symbols I saw in the domed room Atlantean?"

Hermes glanced at Antinous and nodded. They both looked pleased. I think I finally passed a test.

With the grace of an athlete, Antinous rose from the table and returned with a package about the size of a laptop but much thicker. More like a heavy atlas. I wondered wildly for a moment if it were a suitcase bomb.

"The Cosmic Code must never fall into the wrong hands, my daughter. The power must be protected until the world is ready."

On cue from Hermes, Antinous reverently folded the soft antelope skin back. A tablet of polished green faience covered in Greek script glowed as if lighted from within. I recognized it immediately from my Abydos dream.

And the following to be the truth.
That which is below is like that which is above,
and that which is above is like that which is below,
in the accomplishment of the miracle of one thing.
And as all things came from the One, through the meditation of the One,
so all things were born from one thing by adaptation.

I read quickly. Above and below reflecting each other like a cosmic mirror. Macrocosm and microcosm.

"What is the One?" I asked.

"Everything comes from the One Energy—both what you see around you and what you cannot see. We may seem separate, but only the form changes, not the essence. We all come from the One. We are all one."

"But if you know the secret to the cosmos," I asked, "why do you not just manifest a way out of the danger?"

"I have manifested, Isenkhebe. I have manifested the Emerald Tablet, and I have manifested you."

Hermes swallowed my hand in his. How unlike his touch was from that of my mother Sit-hathor with the Hathor energy that aroused in me a hot frenzy. His energy flowed into me and filled me with calm.

"You are the chosen one, my daughter. It is your destiny to protect the Tablet."

Hermes squeezed my hand harder. A slight buzz in my ears grew louder. I had no sense of my body. I no longer felt the chair. I no longer saw Hermes or Antinous, although I was vaguely aware of the oil lamps casting shadows on the rows and rows of scrolls. I drifted outside of time in a velvet sea—just as I had in my living room the first night with the Red Mirror.

"Surely you recognize your unique power, Isenkhebe."

Hermes' voice swam through deep water to my ear.

I'd never thought myself powerful, but I was here; I had passed through the Red Mirror to this life. That must be unique. It certainly couldn't be common. I had another power, too. The Hathor Power.

"You must take the Emerald Tablet out of Egypt. There is very little time."

When Hermes squeezed my fingers again, I came back to my chair. The world returned once more to sharp focus.

He hesitated, looked over at Antinous, and then back at me. This time he took my hand in both of his. His tone was soft and patient, like a doctor giving a patient startling news and trying to deliver it in the gentlest way possible.

"You shall be the wife of Antinous; he will take you home to Greece. Your new Greek name is *Isidora*, gift of Isis. All has been arranged."

Wife? I would've pulled my hand away if Hermes hadn't held it tight.

"A woman cannot travel alone. A woman cannot live alone," he said patiently. "This you know to be true."

What I knew is that I didn't know the Greek, at all. He was handsome, even beautiful, but cold and aloof. I sensed wariness on his part. How convinced was he of this marriage?

As uncommon as it was for a man not to desire me, I couldn't see that he was in the least attracted to me. His eyes told me nothing.

Would he expect me to be faithful to him? Surely they both understood that impossible for a priestess of Hathor. And I wanted River God. I still held out hope.

River God. Would I ever see him again—in this life or the other?

Hermes claimed to know the secret to the cosmos, the Cosmic Code. He must understand how souls could meet each other on both sides of the Red Mirror.

"Hermes, have we known each other before? Will we know each other again?"

If he thought it odd that I so abruptly changed the subject, he didn't show it. He might even have expected my question. If we are all one, he might be able to read my thoughts. Qeb-ha managed to probe quite deep into my mind, and his powers seemed feeble compared to the genius of Hermes Trismegistus.

"We shall know each other until we have learned what we need to learn," he answered.

Elaine had said the same thing to me when I called her to ask about reincarnation. Until Hermes, she'd been the only person I knew who believed in souls meeting again and again through time.

But Hermes Thrice-Greatest had an even more complex notion of past and future lives.

"Do not think, my daughter, in terms of have known or will know; they exist at the same moment. Time is a continuum that loops back on itself."

Antinous had said nothing all this time. What secrets did *he* know? I still couldn't read anything in his eyes. His face was a mask.

I sighed. My choices weren't limited; I had none. I resigned myself to what must be rather than what I wanted. The fortune-teller at Carla's party had been perfectly clear. If I were to save Isis, then I must leave Egypt at once.

"When do we sail?"

Chapter 21 Antinous

I followed Antinous up the spiral staircase, each of us with a torch. Neither of us spoke; I could only guess what was going through his mind. The tension between us was electric. We hurried down the long tunnel, but he stopped at the bottom of the steps that lead up to the little chapel with the false door.

The torches in our hands blew a little sidewise. After the stuffiness of the damp tunnel, the air seemed almost fresh.

Antinous stood inches away. White Atlantean symbols danced against the blue dome behind his head. He smelled of lamp oil and slightly of male sweat, without any hint of perfumed oils or myrrh. His skin glowed. I'd never seen a man so perfectly formed.

His eyes were the color of the sky over Thebes on a spring morning. His lashes were thick like brushes. Leather bands encircled his wrists; he wore no other adornment and no *kohl* around his eyes.

The gold highlights in his curls shimmered in a halo around his Adonis face. His lower lip was slightly fuller than the upper, which was shaped into a bow; his mouth almost formed a pout. His chin had a deep cleft. A muscle in his jaw knotted and unknotted.

Antinous didn't speak; he didn't move. My breasts rose and fell as I breathed; the sheer linen clung to their curve. The emerald eyes of the serpents coiling around my arms glinted in the torchlight when

I reached out to trace my long nail around his lips.

He put his free hand on the nape of my neck. His grip was more forceful than I had expected; it didn't fit with his aloof demeanor. His eyes locked on mine, but I saw none of the hunger I see in men's eyes.

My fingers combed through the short curls on his neck. I traced around his ear with my fingertips. My eyes invited him.

Finally he lowered his face toward me, but didn't close his eyes until his lips were on mine. His tongue went deep; he penetrated me as far as he could. I opened my lips and took him in, sucking on his tongue, urging him on. My heart raced; heat surged through my veins. I felt hot as the sun.

He was rock hard and big enough to please anyone. I cupped my hand around the swollen bulge of his *chiton*, leaning into him, rubbing my breasts against his chest, pressing my thighs into his.

How far were we from the wall? I envisioned my back against the cool damp stone, one hand guiding his steel rod to my wet chamber, the other holding a torch. Would the torches stay lit if we lay them down on the stone floor?

But instead of responding to me, he drew back while still gripping my neck. He pulled his lips away in the middle of the kiss and left me with my lips open, swollen, hungry for more.

His manhood slowly shriveled until I finally dropped my hand to hang awkwardly at my side. His eyes stayed locked with mine, but they revealed no secrets; they told me nothing about what was going on behind them. It was as if their blue depths had no connection to the changes in his body.

The torches in our hands burned evenly in the still air. There wasn't a sound in the domed chamber except our breathing.

He was my husband and my future. With the tip of my index finger, the one that traced his ear, I eased the strap of my dress aside. Slowly, deliberately, oozing with promise, I revealed each seductive inch of bare flesh. My breast was a pale mound in the yellow light, the dark nipple erect and throbbing.

Antinous looked down, blinked once and then looked into my face. Taking his hand away from the nape of my neck, he slid the sheer fabric back into place, covering me, never taking his eyes away from mine.

I jerked as if he had slapped me.

He switched the torch to my right hand and then took my left hand into his right.

"Come." He said nothing more, but gripped my hand just as firmly as he had gripped the back of my neck and started up the stairs.

Antinous dropped my hand once we reached the top of the steps and entered the chapel. He didn't speak or touch me again but walked quickly with eyes straight ahead.

Goliath still waited outside the double wooden doors. He must have heard us on the other side, because he stood at attention when we exited. He looked sharply at Antinous and then directly at me, something he rarely did. He judged the danger to me by a brief glance at my face. I may have shown discomfort, but not fear.

We returned to my chambers in silence. Antinous led the way; I followed him, with Goliath in the rear. I replayed the scene in the tunnel over and over in my head.

He had kissed me. I had responded. Were we not to be husband and wife? Had I violated some Greek taboo at the foot of the stairs?

Maia must have sent for Qeb-ha, because he waited in my chambers. His face, usually placid and round as a Buddha, was marred with worry lines. Both he and Maia were surprised to see Antinous but concealed it well. I introduced him as Hermes' assistant. Nothing more.

Goliath kept his eye on Antinous and his hand on the hilt of his short-sword. Shame washed over me that I ever entertained thoughts of abusing him. The Nubian was wholly devoted to me and totally at my mercy. I would have made him miserable for my own pleasure. He, my savior, the one who first found me in the desert and cradled me like a child—the first man to touch me after my escape, after the General.

Maia's eyes moved from me to Antinous and back again. She took in every detail of his tall frame and golden curls. She saw his beauty and bearing, and she knows me.

I could see her thinking, *Who is this new lover?* I kept my face a mask.

"Hermes will send you a message very soon," Antinous said in the flat tone of a messenger with no personal interest in the message.

"Do not go, Antinous. I wish to speak with you."

"Please leave us," I told the others.

Qeb-ha hesitated for the slightest of moments, then bowed his head, leading Maia from the room. Goliath went no further than just outside the door; his giant frame cast a shadow across the threshold.

Antinous leaned against the railing of my balcony, his elbow on the edge. His stance appeared relaxed, but not his face. As in the tunnel, the muscle knotted and unknotted in his jaw.

"I do not consider it safe to talk here," he said.

"Am I not to know our plan, Antinous? I do not think myself unreasonable. My life is at stake, after all."

I moved closer to him, and he shifted his weight; I could see he was very ill at ease. His jaw set. The cleft in his chin deepened. For a brief moment, I thought he wouldn't tell me the plan for my own escape. I had an almost irresistible urge to slap him.

When he spoke, his voice was so low I had to move right next to him. Again I smelled the faint scent of male mixed with burnt oil.

"Speak of this to no one, Isenkhebe. Do you agree?"

How could he think me so foolish?

No. He was right to caution me. I would have told Qeb-ha; I would have told Maia.

"A Phoenician ship waits at Rosetta, where the Nile meets the sea. We must sail north from Saïs without detection." Antinous stood erect now, tense all over.

"Tell no one," he repeated.

He started again to leave, and again I stopped him. This time I put my hand on his forearm. His skin was pale next to mine. Even the tiny hairs on his arm were so fair they almost disappeared. He felt warm, but not damp.

"Antinous, did I offend you in the tunnel? Do you not desire me?"

It took some courage for me to ask. But if Antinous was one of those Greeks who favor male friends over a wife, I wanted to know now.

He stared out at the temple grounds for a long moment. Ra was sinking towards the west, and the heat of the day had finally broken. Birds flocked around the myrtle tree blooming a few yards away; a peacock trilled his mating call. The high tinkling sounds of women's laughter carried across the garden like musical notes from a glass wind chime.

My breath caught when he turned his eyes back to me. They were exactly the same color as the sky behind him, and in them I saw the yearning and hunger I am accustomed to see in men's eyes. I also saw doubt.

"I know you can satisfy me, Isenkhebe. But can I satisfy you?"

Night came without a message from Hermes. I felt danger all around me; I knew I was running out of time.

My nerves were the frayed ends of electrical wires with live current sparking out. A warm bath did nothing. The song of the nightingales did nothing. The breeze rustling through the palm fronds did nothing. Not the sweet scents of jasmine, not the heady waft of myrrh, there was nothing that could soothe me. Maia brought me a draught of potent herbs to help me sleep.

I needed a man's arms around me, a man with two daggers, one sharp and within reach at the side of the bed. Goliath was no longer an option. I couldn't use him or any slave for my own pleasure—not after the desert.

Chapter 22 The Commander

A hand pressed down on my mouth. I tried to sit up, but couldn't move my head. There was no moon. I could see nothing in the darkness except the form of a man directly over me. I kicked, and I thrashed, but could not dislodge him. Bile came up into my mouth.

"Sh-h-h, Isis," River God breathed in my ear.

I clutched him to me, digging my fingertips into his muscled back, hoping to draw strength from his power. His lips replaced his hand, and he tried to kiss me, but I sobbed too hard.

I felt his muscles tighten over the full length of my body. I wanted to melt into him, to become one with him. I could walk out of here, and no one would see me.

River God waited for me to calm. His lips and tongue traveled slowly down my neck, across the hollow of my throat and up to my ear. He took the lobe between his teeth, gently, and then sucked with long languid pulls that I felt right down to my throbbing lotus. His lips were hot and moist.

His fingers went in my mouth, stroking my tongue, wetting them before going to my swollen breast to stroke my nipple in small gentle circles. My saliva was slick on the throbbing tip.

His tongue was in my ear; he breathed life into me. He took his time, unhurried, savoring my need. His touch caressed me as tenderly as a breeze. My breath was so shallow, I scarcely took in air.

He ran his tongue around my ear and licked down my neck. His finger massaged my lotus in his slow, languid rhythm that teased me to life, but never hurried to finish.

No one had a touch like River God.

My hand found his hardness; I felt him swell as I squeezed the first droplets of wet from the tip. The head was moist and smooth in my palm. I licked my hand and made him wetter still, rubbing his bulb with gentle circles, caressing his shaft in my hot palm, pumping up and down, up and down, slowly, slowly, until he grew hard as the stone phallus of Min.

He moaned. The sound of his pleasure was sweeter than the softest love song. The muscles in his thighs and butt grew hard and taut like carved marble. I sucked on his navel, exploring deep with my tongue. Then like a preening cat, I licked his hard nipples until he pulled my face up and finally kissed me, his tongue plunging to my throat, his lips pressing on mine, devouring me.

He was almost, but not quite, brutal. The palm of his hand crushed along my ribs, across my soft belly and dug into my mound. I opened up to him.

His fingers slid up the dark damp and pushed against my cervix. My wetness soaked the bed linen. I whimpered at each stroke, spreading my loins, shifting my hips to open wider, to welcome his touch, to give him everything.

When his lips left mine and began their trail of kisses to my breast, I arched my back, raising my throbbing nipples to his lips, begging for his mouth, aching to be suckled.

His tongue was wet and warm when he sucked. His teeth brought me to the edge of pain but never took me there, always hovering at the extreme threshold of pleasure and not crossing over. I gripped his head and pressed him into me, but he moved to my other nipple and teased with his teeth and wet tongue.

My hips rose and fell as his fingers possessed me, plunging into my wet, rotating on my lotus, exploring every part of my dark valley.

I rocked on the palm of his hand.

My cries must have wakened the household, but Maia didn't come. She knew those sounds well. Pehtes curled at the top of my bare scalp, purring a lion's roar, wallowing in the animal scent.

The sleeping potion fogged my senses. I floated above the bed yet could still feel his touch. The night stars disappeared; the open balcony faded. Las Vegas sparkled through the tall windows of the Wynn.

In one breath, he was River God, in the next, Rasheed. Our souls glided back and forth between two worlds.

"Why did you not come back to me?" I whispered. "I came back for you."

Of course, he thought I meant I came back from the desert and not through the Red Mirror. River God knew nothing about the future. He stopped his caress and let his hand rest on my thigh for just a moment until he rolled onto his back.

"I came for you in the desert," he said in a flat, cold voice.

He put his hands behind his head. He looked up and not at me.

"But you allowed Hetmus-hor to take me from Goliath," I pleaded. "It could have been you. It *should* have been you."

He got up from bed. The spell was broken, like the night of the bath in Thebes. Words are always the spoiler with River God.

His silhouette against the open night sky moved quietly in the room to find his sandals and his sword.

"You must leave Saïs," he said. "It is not safe for you, even here in the Temple."

I listened to his voice in the dark, telling me the real reason he had come.

"I have heard rumors at Court. The Persians will pay any price for your capture. Cambyses wants revenge for General Sher's death."

I closed my eyes and saw the General's startled face, eyes huge with disbelief, blood gushing from his slit throat and spilling onto my hands. I went icy cold. The Persians are masters of torture. It takes days for their victims to die.

The fortune-teller's warning screamed in my ears. *You have to go back, Isis, or you will suffer. You can't imagine the suffering.*

River God sat on the edge of the bed. I couldn't make out his features in the dark, but I clearly heard his worry.

"I fear the Crown Prince and his vile Scribe are scheming to trade you when Cambyses invades. There are whispers of an arrest warrant."

An elephant stepped on my chest. I had thought the danger was from the Persians, but I wasn't safe even from Egyptians.

"You must leave for the South, maybe as far as Kush."

"I cannot go south."

River God gripped my shoulders and pulled me into him. I winced from the pain of his fingers digging into my flesh. His eyes flashed in the dark.

"You will do exactly as I say. Do you hear me? This is no time for your foolishness."

River God still thought of me as the pampered party girl I once was, but I was not the same woman. I had survived the desert. I had survived the General.

"Make ready to leave at sunset tomorrow," he ordered in his Commander's tone. "Look for a ship under my banner."

River God didn't know the Persians would drive deep into Egypt, that not even Kush would be safe, but I did. I knew how the war ended. I had seen it from the future.

"The Persians will invade in the month of Payni," I said. Maybe that little piece of information would save him.

"So soon! How do you know this? Has the priest Qeb-ha seen it in the Temple?"

River God certainly had great faith in his gods.

I took his hand in mine and covered my mouth with it, drinking in his fragrance, tasting my own fluids. He pulled away gently and raised my fingers to his own mouth. His breath was hot; the tip of his tongue wet my fingertips.

Was this the last time in this life I would feel his lips on me?

I had said nothing at all to him about Antinous and Greece; I couldn't. It was too dangerous to tell anyone, even River God. One could never tell what one didn't know. Even under torture. So I lied to him with my silence.

"Make yourself ready," and not "I love you," were his last words as he headed toward the balcony.

"Why do you always leave me?" I cried out as he slipped over the side and was gone into the night.

Maia came to me while I still slept. The Sun God Ra had barely risen; the trees were full of morning birdsong. She knelt on the yellow-and-green striped carpet beside my bed when I opened my eyes.

"What is it? You are frightening me. Tell me at once!"

"Isenkhebe Nefrusobek has not had her monthly bleeding."

I looked at her, stupefied. Of course, she would know that about me. She was responsible for everything that I ate, everything I put on my body. She was responsible for my laundry.

I closed my eyes and unravelled the crazy quilt of what happened when, and on which side of the mirror. I think I had known from the moment I saw Maia's worried face. The General.

"Is it the Persian, Isenkhebe Nefrusobek?"

The possibility clearly terrified her. She would consider any child as sacrilege, but the bastard of a foreigner growing in an Egyptian priestess would be beyond bearing.

I didn't answer. I lay very still with my eyes closed.

"Isenkhebe Nefrusobek cannot carry this child. The father is a monster; the child will be an abomination, cursed by the Gods. We must do something now. This morning. It will be over in a few hours."

"No! I cannot be weakened in any way today."

Maia knew then that I was leaving. And as I hadn't revealed my plans to her, she also knew I was leaving her behind. Her eyes were wet and her hand trembled when she pressed a small vial into my palm.

"Take five drops each morning, three days in a row. It will be slower, but as effective."

Finally the message from Hermes arrived. Sunset. Be ready at sunset.

The day passed in sadness and good-byes. I stroked Pehtes who, sensing change, never left my side. I considered taking her with me; a Greek woman raised in Cyrene on the Libyan coast might have a cat named Pehtes, Berber for "the black one." But I knew I must leave her behind.

I touched each piece of my jewelry, so beautifully crafted in gold, silver and electrum, and then opened each of my precious scrolls with their exquisite hieroglyphs in black and red ink. The medical papyrus contained a useless section on women.

Prescription to make a woman cease to become pregnant for one, two or three years: Grind together finely a measure of acacia dates with honey. Moisten seed-wool with the mixture and insert into the vagina.

Too late for that.

The steel blade of my jeweled dagger was still razor sharp; again I saw dark red blood flowing from the General's throat and shocked betrayal in his eyes. His death haunted me. The desert haunted me. Were the charioteer and the horses still buried in the sand? Would their bodies mummify in the arid river bed to be discovered thousands of years from now?

In the end, I couldn't part with my necklace from the hunt—the one from the General's tent. I held it in the sunlight; tiny golden rays reflected off the delicate charms.

A vulture saved me from the cobra in the desert. The General gave me my first clue to his black heart when he took a crocodile between his thick fingers. I smiled at the fertile rabbits and thought of the General's seed growing inside me. Would I allow his child to live?

I could seduce Antinous as soon as possible and claim the child as his—or I could tell him the truth. A fine start to a marriage already in peril. My options were all painful. The General managed to hold me prisoner even after his death.

I called Qeb-ha and Maia to my bedchamber and gave them pouches filled with amulets and jewelry.

"We must not travel together," I explained in the calmest voice I could muster. "You will need these for bribes."

"Please give this to my mother," I told Qeb-ha.

His old eyes filled with tears when he saw the small box with my Hathor lapis lazuli ring, the one identical to Sit-hathor's, one of two in all Egypt.

"It is too dangerous for me to have it on my person. You understand that, Qeb-ha, do you not?"

He gripped my hand and didn't try to stop his tears from flowing.

I remembered that first day in Sit-hathor's temple when he had waited for me in the shade among columns with heads of Hathor carved at their tops. I had despised his high eunuch voice then; now I yearned for the sound of it, never to stop hearing it.

"Thank you, Qeb-ha, my companion and brother. We shall all meet in Thebes. Then I shall go south to Elephantine and further to Kush, if I sense danger."

He knew I didn't speak the truth, but chose to say nothing. *The fate and the fortune that come, it is the Gods that send them.*

Ra was sliding toward nightfall; the fading light turned the rose granite walls of the old Pharaoh's *naos* a golden red. Birds feeding on evening insects raised a deafening chorus. The heat of the day had passed. River God waited for me at the wharf to sail south, not knowing about Antinous and Greece, not knowing I would never come.

Chapter 23 *Escape*

Goliath was to take me to meet Antinous at the double doors in the Green Chapel. We had just entered the first courtyard when a great weight hit the ground behind me, like the falling of a tree. Goliath lay dead still; blood flowed down his face from under his white linen headdress.

I went to my knees to help him, but a hand came from behind and stuffed a cloth into my mouth. I tried to lash out; iron arms held me in place. A rough sack went over my head, but not before I saw the flash of red turban.

The sack had held grain; I breathed chaff up my nose. I gagged. Vomit came into my throat and then was sucked into my lungs. It would be a strange end indeed if I choked to death in a filthy bag before the Persians could capture me, before the Crown Prince could arrest me, before I could escape with the Emerald Tablet.

Hands lifted up the sack and tossed me over a shoulder. I hung upside down and jostled wildly as my captor ran. The bag bound me as tight a swaddled infant. With no way to kick or punch, I rolled my body back and forth, trying to throw him off balance. But I was helpless.

We fell. I hit the ground with a smack. I could see nothing but willed my body to roll sideways, over and over. I felt soft grass instead of stone and heard scuffling, but no voices. My hands were not bound; I ripped at the sack to free myself.

I was picked up again, higher in the air, by a taller man who ran with long strides. I struggled even harder. My new captor entered a building. I sensed he was alone; his footsteps and movements were the only sound.

The filthy sack was pulled off me, and the cloth came out of my mouth; my vomit stained it. I gulped air. When I no longer felt sick, I dared look up.

Hetmus-hor towered over me. I was as stunned as the day he appeared in the desert with Goliath and River God. I threw my arms around his neck, sobbing with relief. Hetmus the Savoir—again. He crushed me to him with such force that I thought my ribs would break, but never have I so enjoyed pain.

"They said you were in the south. Qeb-ha said you were forbidden to come to me."

"I told you that I'd do whatever it takes to have you, Isis. *Qualquier cosa.*"

I had heard those exact words before—at Carla's penthouse party—the night of the shock of the fortune-teller telling me I had to go back and save myself. I stared into the his red-flecked eyes.

"Hector?"

"*Sí*, Isis, it is me."

A child at Christmas couldn't have been more filled with wonder. For Hetmus-hor to appear suddenly in the temple grounds to save me was a miracle. But never in my wildest imaginings could I dream of Argentinean Hector from Las Vegas to be here.

"How, Hector? How are you here?"

"Your *amiga* Barb told me everything. When I crossed through the Red Mirror, I—or am I Hetmus now?—came as fast as I could."

Hector had come through the Red Mirror! I struggled to process first that he was able to pass through—that I wasn't the only one who could—and then that he did it for me.

"Did you think I would let you face this alone, Isis? You do not know me at all."

He kissed me lightly, holding my chin with those long fingers that know just where to find my burning G-Spot. His brilliant white smile flashed again. "But you will."

Shouts rang out. I couldn't tell if the men were outside or inside the temple. The thunder of feet pounding stone paths reached us even through the thick walls. I thought I felt the earth quake under the weight of an army invading the temple grounds.

"Royal Guards are searching everywhere for you; they were at your chambers when I arrived there not an hour ago."

Gentle Maia. Old Qeb-ha. Vomit came up in my mouth again.

They would be forced to tell everything. But the Prince and his evil Scribe would never believe they didn't know my plans. I rocked against Hector, my face in his chest, my eyes squeezed shut in a vain attempt to push the nightmare visions of their agony from my mind.

I understood then how right Antinous had been that I must tell no one.

"There is nothing you can do for them, Isis." Hector shook me gently to bring me back. "We must get out of here now, Isis. Now."

Just knowing me was a death sentence. What would they do to *me* if captured?

"I have to get to the ship! I must meet Antinous. Only he knows the way to the port through the underground tunnels. Only he knows the plan."

"Antinous?" Hector's smile dimmed. "Who is Antinous?"

I put my hand on his bronzed forearm, just above the gold armband; he was warm, and his skin moist. I felt suddenly and inexplicably calm. The Universe had sent Hector to me. I was going to make it.

"There is too much to explain now, Hector, but Antinous will take me out of Egypt. It is the only way I shall be safe."

Hector rolled back onto his haunches and stared at me. The sparkle in his eyes was gone. I don't think saving me for someone else is what he envisioned when he went through the Red Mirror.

But he stood up, took my hand and pulled me with no effort to my feet.

"Then let us find Antinous."

The tall double doors were closed and locked. No Antinous. We stared at the long empty hallway with no place to hide. We waited, exposed and vulnerable. I tried to control my panic.

Hector leaned against the stone wall next to the doors. I finally noticed the blood on his iron thrusting sword.

"Goliath, the Nubian? Is he dead? Please tell me that he is not dead."

Last I saw Goliath he lay in a pool of his own blood, his headdress bright white against the dark red. I never tasted his manhood, but I kissed with sheer joy his dusty black feet in the desert. They were the most wonderful sight I had ever seen.

"The Nubian is a giant; he will live, but the Arabs are dead. I recognized the one in the red turban. He was with you in the desert when we found you."

The Arabs from the desert! They must be working for the Persians—or even the Crown Prince or his Scribe. And they had dared enter the sacred grounds of the Temple. I was surrounded by enemies. River God was right; I wasn't safe anywhere in Saïs.

I pounded on the wooden door. Nothing. I pounded even harder. Still no response. But when I raised my fist for the third time, the door opened. The same old priest stood with a torch in his hand.

He still didn't speak. He looked up at Hector, appraised him quickly, and stepped aside. The door shut behind us, and he bolted it.

"Where is Antinous?" I cried out. I was losing my battle with panic.

His shaved head bobbed up and down; the ankhs in his earlobes swung back and forth. He handed Hector the torch and began speaking with his hands. Sign language! My Greek tutors had overlooked that.

"He says Antinous left to go to your quarters."

I looked at Hector in wonder. "You know sign language?"

"*Sí*, although I am not sure how. I am not quite used to being Hetmus." The twinkle was back in his eye, the charm in his smile.

Footsteps rang in the corridor on the other side of the doors. Not a few men, but many. Then came pounding with metal shields or the hilts of swords. We stared at the bolt rocking back and forth for a heartbeat—and then ran.

We no longer cared if they could hear us. It was a race to get through the secret door before they burst through the others.

The priest pulled on the lever at the base of the false stone door. The crack in the corner opened an inch at a time. I thought my heart would burst from my chest. We slid through the narrow gap, and Hector leaned against the stone slab to close it. There was the sucking sound of an airtight lock. Then we could see no trace of the opening, at least not from our side.

"Someone must tell Antinous to meet us at the river," I whispered in terror.

Hector and the priest spoke with their hands. I looked from one to the other and then at the wall, expecting it to move at any moment.

The priest's face was solemn but held no fear. He took off the gold cord with the ankh key and handed it to Hector.

"The priest will wait for Antinous," Hector said.

"Thank you!" I kissed the paper-thin skin of the priest's ancient hand. "Thank you!"

We could hear the muffled sounds of shouting and clanging metal on the other side of the wall. Hector grabbed my hand and took three steps at a time. I couldn't keep up.

He scooped me into his arms and was at an ebony door within seconds, but not the same door with seven-pointed star that led to Hermes and the library.

The priest nodded his head from the halo of his torch at the top of the steps. His giant ankh earrings swung erratically about his short neck in staccato bursts of light.

Hector inserted the key into the lock, and the door swung open into absolute blackness. He looked around the blue room, stood me to my feet, and grabbed the only torch. We stepped through, and the door slammed behind us.

On the other side was silence and unending black. We ran down the damp tunnel toward nothingness, our lone torch spluttering wildly.

I struggled to keep up with his long stride. My sandals flopped and slid on my feet.

He stopped, not winded at all, passed the torch into my hand, and picked me up. My knees bent over his forearms; I hooked my arm around the back of his neck.

Hector moved quite fast now. We sped through the tunnel; his paces were long and steady. He may have been the spoiled son of a rich man, but he kept himself in shape.

The tunnel took a sharp turn and sloped upward, the incline not steep, but definitely heading to the surface. We ended abruptly at a small wooden door, rounded at the top, bolted on our side.

Hector set me down, signaled for me to move backwards with the torch, and slowly slid the bolt open with only the slightest squeak.

Fresh air poured into the tunnel. The wind had come up since sunset; the flame of the torch bent sideways. It was dark outside but not as black as the tunnel. The sky over the harbor lingered between twilight and night.

Hector showed me a special knock, a pattern of hard and soft. I was to bolt the door and stay inside. An eternity passed while I waited. At last the knocks came, and I opened the bolt. Hector stepped in and quickly closed the door.

"We are just across from the wharf. Soldiers are everywhere. There is a warship moored at the far end of the quay. It flies the banner of the Commander of the Armies. No soldiers approach it but swarm over all other boats."

"The ship is for me to escape to the south." I gripped his forearm with all my strength.

"But my only hope is north to the sea, to Rosetta."

This time we stepped through the round-top wooden door together. I was not prepared for the numbers of men in uniform. What had I done to deserve so much attention?

The General's dead eyes stared at me from a pool of dark blood flowing from his throat, and I knew. One does not kill a Persian general without being hunted.

We stood in the shelter of the doorway for a few brief moments. My hands trembled. I saw soldiers everywhere, but not close by. Hector stepped outside and kept his back to the wall. I watched his tall figure move away from me before I dared step out myself.

A hand came out of the night and closed over my mouth. I started to scream, but stopped; I wanted no attention drawn to me. An arm pushed me back into the dark recess around the door. I struggled, but the man held me fast. Who now?

A halo of pale curls glowed in the lights of the harbor. I bobbed my head up and down rapidly, relaxing my body to let him know I recognized him, and his hand dropped from my mouth.

"Antinous!" My voice was a breathless whisper. "How did you find me?"

"Hermes. He has always said that we would meet here."

Hector didn't make a sound when he came up behind Antinous, but his long shadow fell across the wall behind me. Antinous pivoted to face the Egyptian, drawing a sword as he turned. I grabbed his wrist to keep him from striking.

"No, Antinous! He saved my life. But for him, I would not be here."

There was a long moment of tension, no one speaking, the two men staring at each other, measuring the other's worth. My left hand on Hector's arm and my right on Antinous burned as if I touched fire.

I sensed that Antinous sized up one of my lovers with whom he must compete. Hector judged the man who would take me from him.

Finally, Hector said begrudgingly, "Greek, you are the luckiest man alive."

Then he smiled at me in the most sweet and tender way and put his palm on my cheek. His love flowed into me, giving me strength.

"Let us get you on that ship."

Antinous carried a hemp sack with green wool, lengths of silken cord, and a Greek wig. I took off my black waves with gold ankhs and pulled the dark blonde plaits and curls over my shaved head.

While Antinous sorted the yards of wool fabric, Hector wiped *kohl* and mica from my eyes and eyebrows with my Egyptian linen gown. Then he took the green *peplos* cloth from Antinous and draped it around me expertly, fastening it in place with the pins and silk cords. When he saw my surprise, he smiled.

"Hetmus-hor knew a few Greek ladies in his day," he said through a blaze of white teeth.

I went in a sack again, but not upside down. I should not make a sound; no one must suspect anything. We hurried along the barricade wall, keeping to the shadows. I bounced in the sack and held my body in a tight fetal position. We left the search behind. The night grew quieter.

Hector laid me gently on the ground. His sandals crunched on the loose rock as he walked away. I heard only one set of footsteps; Antinous stayed with me, but neither of us spoke. He was here; he had lived up to his promise, but more than ever I was aware of his doubt. And he didn't even know about the General's child.

Chapter 24 The Great Green

Gentle waves lapped against the stone wharf a few yards away. Humming insects swarmed in the cool of the night. Night birds called from the trees. I barely breathed; my breasts did not move.

Footsteps approached, and Hector heaved me up high again, over his shoulder. We left the gravel walkway and made little sound, only leather soles slapping on hard pavement. We crossed open ground; I thought us very close to the river. I heard the ponderous creak of a wooden ship against the stone quay.

Antinous walked beside Hector, matching his stride. Then Hector went ahead of Antinous and the sound was leather on wood. We took three steps down before stopping.

Quiet words were exchanged. I heard River God's voice, low, giving orders. The footfalls on the deck of the ship sounded hollow; there must be a space below. We descended a short flight of steps, very steep. I could hear the river rushing past the cedar boards, then someone untied the sack and it fell around my ankles.

River God reeled with shock. I had forgotten I wore the dress and wig of a Greek and no black *kohl* on my eyes. My naked face must have been pale as white sand in moonlight.

"Do not utter one word." His tone chilled me. "The sound of a woman's voice on this ship will carry all the way to the Crown

Prince's ear."

His voice was cold. There was no affection at all in his eyes. Was it only last night that he caressed me with such tenderness?

How could I beg him to take me to the sea, if I couldn't speak? His face was black with jealousy and rage, but I saw longing under his anger. This time I was leaving him.

We stood in a tight circle, the four of us—blond and muscular Antinous, Hector so tall he could not stand fully upright in the low space, and fuming River God, rigid and tense in his military vest with the Pharaoh's golden insignia. And me, facing the three men who controlled my destiny.

Hector held out his right arm to River God.

"We are agreed? You will take Isis and the Greek north to meet the Phoenician ship."

At first River God refused to look Hector in the eye. When he finally faced him, he didn't try to conceal his contempt for the man who had lost me in the desert and then was praised as my savior. And now Hector arranged my escape, but not to the south as River God planned.

Hector gripped River God's shoulder; his long fingers dug into the hard muscle. I thought for a moment he might shake him, as if to bring him to his senses.

"I know exactly what I ask of you, man. But there is no other way."

I actually thought River God would refuse. The muscles in his jaw were so knotted I could see them flex even in the poor light. His left eye twitched in a tic.

"Do you think I would give her up," Hector insisted, "if I thought there was any chance I could have her?"

River God glared up at Hector; his black eyes were hard as obsidian. I thought him so handsome, but tonight the bones of his face formed harsh, ugly angles. His mouth, so lush when he kissed me, was tight and cruel.

I held my breath. I think we all held our breaths. At last, he gripped Hector's forearm, just below the elbow, and laid his left hand on Hector's shoulder to signal the pact. A man of his word, River God would not betray his pledge.

The air in the narrow space below deck was as charged as before a sandstorm. My heart raced, and my head pounded from the suspense.

Antinous stood silently to one side, almost out of the ring of light. He was no fool. He understood the drama he witnessed and the role he played. One wrong word from him and this scene could end in tragedy.

Hector stroked my cheek with the back of his fingers. The red specks in his eyes were iridescent. I couldn't look away from them.

"I shall never find another woman like you, Isis."

Then he kissed me, long and deep. He didn't hurry. He was oblivious to River God and Antinous standing next to us. When he pulled away, he leaned down and whispered in my ear.

"You owe me one. *Hasta Las Vegas.*"

He kissed me one last time, lightly, just a fleeting touch of his lips, and then disappeared up the steps.

River God stood absolutely frozen, like a quartzite statue in a tomb. When he finally looked at me, his glare was full of accusation. I saw betrayal in his face and wounded pride. I hadn't said anything to him about Greece—or Antinous, whom he ignored. He wouldn't look in the Greek's direction. Raw pain sharpened the planes of his face.

I wanted to reach out and tell him this was not goodbye. I wanted to say the words he had said to me in Las Vegas, *We have known each other before, and we will know each other again.*

But River God knew nothing of the future; he knew nothing of himself as Rasheed.

This was the last time I would see him in this life. I edged close to him, my body yielding, his more rigid than ever. I was desperate to reach him, so I did what I'd never before done with a lover. I summoned the Power.

My skin flushed with heat. A hot aura pulsed from my body. I believe my flesh glowed in the dim light.

"You told me in Thebes that the Gods set us on our separate paths," I crooned in the softest of honey whispers. "This is not the path I would have chosen; this is not the path I want."

Still he didn't respond, not to me, not to the Power.

"I would have lain in your arms until you left me," I breathed. "I would have been there waiting for your return."

Balancing on my tiptoes, my breasts pressing on his leather chest, I put my lips to his. Chiseled from stone by a master sculptor, they did not yield. My desire burned so bright, I would have lain with him right there on the rough planks, even with Antinous standing over us.

His pride wouldn't let him hold me. He stared straight ahead, refusing to look at me, trying to make of me a non-person, to have me no longer exist.

Only the twitch in his eyelid gave him away. He would show no pain or weakness; he cut me out of his heart at the same time he cut my heart out of me.

Invisible fingers tore at the connective tissue in my chest. Not even the Persians could invent such torture.

He moved past me and up the steps, not looking back at me, never looking at Antinous. I couldn't bring myself to look at Antinous.

I leaned my back against a pole and watched my heart, ripped from my chest, pumping on the wood planks, spewing blood, the dark red stain spreading in a wide pool around my feet.

The warship pulled away from the wharf, oars moving crisply in the water. I heard the sail unfurl with a sharp snap, filled instantly by a brisk wind. River God was true to his word; we entered the swift current flowing toward the Great Green.

Antinous and I didn't speak. We didn't look at each other. I curled up on two bales and tried to sleep. I was even more exhausted than in Sit-hathor's tent, after the desert. I wondered how living flesh could endure such tension and pain.

Seagulls woke me. The scent of salt saturated even the stale close air below deck.

Antinous rose and went up the steps without a word or look in my direction. He should never have seen me with River God. Those images would burn forever in his mind. They would burn forever in mine.

He came back after a short while, curls tousled by the sea breeze. His cheeks glowed rosy pink, not the pale ash from months buried among scrolls beneath the Temple. He didn't speak, but motioned for me to get into the sack, and then tied the end and hoisted me onto his shoulder as easily as tall Hector had. That surprised me. I don't know why I thought of Antinous as weak.

I could see nothing, but heard the sharp cries of the gulls and waves from the Mediterranean crashing on rocks. Antinous dropped me down on the deck like a bundle of no value, not hard, but not soft. Did he show the others that the bundle meant nothing, or did he demonstrate what he thought of me?

Rough hands hoisted me over the side. Someone caught the sack and dropped me against hard boards. The dinghy pitched back and forth, banging up against the hull. I was leaving Egypt in a sack.

We rocked on the swells and rowed away from the ship. Another boat approached. Ropes lashed us together amid shouting, and then I was picked up again and tossed to unseen arms. I made out a few words of Phoenician.

When we had sailed a short distance, fingers unloosened the knot and the sack fell away from my head. Antinous pulled me from the bottom of the boat to a seat beside him.

The sailors showed no surprise. Paid to mind their own business, they looked at me briefly and then away. But if stories were told, they would be of a Greek noblewoman, not an Egyptian priestess.

We headed to a massive galley with the face of a giant yellow-and-green sea monster painted on the broad bow. The red sail flapped in an easterly wind. Bobbing like a cork in the rolling waves, we floated in a vast expanse of blue sea and sky. Why do they call it the Great

Green? The water was the dark rich lapis blue of my Hathor ring.

I dared glance at Antinous. He stared at the military ship rocking near the surf at the mouth of the river. His face was devoid of emotion, but I knew his mind whirled. I followed his line of sight and saw the small figure of River God in the prow.

We watched him grow smaller as he watched us row away. He never raised his hand. He never moved. Then he was too far away to see.

When I turned back to Antinous, he was staring at me. For a brief second, I wanted to crawl inside his head and read his thoughts, but I really didn't want to know. I met his eyes with complete frankness.

He had seen me stripped naked of all pride and then cast aside. Completely exposed, I had nothing left to hide, and then remembered the General's seed growing inside me.

They lifted us aboard the ship in a kind of sling. I balanced on the listing deck, slippery with salt spray. Twenty rows of oarsmen, three to a bench, lined each side, shackles binding their ankles. The captain barked orders, and the red square sail billowed against the azure sky.

Antinous and I leaned against the wood railing, a wide space between us. We still didn't speak. I was grateful in the brisk air for the Grecian wool. The shoreline slipped further and further away until it disappeared over the horizon. Goodbye Egypt.

I followed Antinous aft to where the captain's cabin filled the deck. The salt scent of sea mixed with tangy cedar. Small windows high up let in light and air. An ordinary wooden table and two simple chairs stood in the middle of the cedar-paneled room; finely-woven striped carpets covered much of the plank floor. There was one bed built into a narrow box hung with heavy burgundy drapes. Brightly painted chests lined one wall.

"I think it best you restrict yourself to the cabin during the voyage to Cyrene. We want nothing to arouse suspicion. From there we shall book passage on a ship bound for Kos."

I looked around. My new home. I looked at Antinous. My new husband. He avoided eye contact. What kind of honeymoon voyage would this be?

"If you concur, of course," he added, finally looking at me. "It will be only a few days."

At least he considered my opinion.

Antinous placed a clay jar of wine, loaf of brown bread and a hunk of white cheese on the crude table.

"I think we both need food."

His voice had that same flat, detached tone; everything happening had nothing to do with him.

"Do you have the Emerald Tablet?" I asked.

He set the package on the table. It was wrapped in the same antelope skin as in the library. When I folded the corners back, the green faience glowed. Stroking the finely-etched script, I wondered about the power that Hermes believed dwelled there. Would it pass to me now?

"The chest with green markings contains clothing."

Antinous indicated a rectangular cedar box painted with the geometric patterns of Greek vases.

The chest was filled with a rainbow of cloth and several blond wigs in Greek style. A leather pouch lay on top. I opened it—a glint of gold—Greek jewelry.

I turned to Antinous and smiled. The corners of his mouth turned up, not a real smile, but still progress. I took hope. The tension in the cabin eased ever so slightly.

"The chest beside it is also for you."

I opened the red lid to dozens of scrolls and turned again, my smile bigger.

"Thank you."

He took a swallow of wine and looked back at me over the rim of the cup. The ice in his eyes melted a degree.

"Hermes sent you a gift."

A large rectangle leaned against the cabin wall. I lifted the drape of blue cloth with silver stars. The heavy wood frame was painted a deep red, but there were no flowers; they must have come later. The mirror itself was polished bronze. I stroked the frame and fingered each silver strut. Brand new.

"Hermes made it for you. He said you would understand."

The Red Mirror. Above and below, past and future, reflecting back on each other. Hermes *Trismegistus*, Hermes Thrice-Greatest, had given me the way home.

Chapter 25 *Antinous Thrice-Greatest*

Antinous spent the rest of the day on deck, leaving me alone in the cabin. I could hardly move in the yards of fabric hanging from my body. Surely Greek women sometimes wear gowns less cumbersome and not wool. I rummaged through the green chest until I found a simple caftan of pale yellow linen.

A large clay *amphora* contained fresh water, on the cold side, but it would do for a sponge bath. I looked in the chest for cleansing oils and found a new copper razor. I would let the hair grow on my head; Greek women don't usually wear wigs. But what body hair did they shave? I'd have to ask Antinous. My tutors hadn't included Greek hygiene in their curriculum.

The leather pouch held three short necklaces exquisitely crafted in gold, with no beads or precious stones. One had tiny owl charms; one was made of links shaped into oak leaves. The third was a heavy thick chain trimmed with scores of delicate tassels.

But I chose my piece with golden vultures, crocodiles and rabbits. A string of lucky charms, it represented overcoming all obstacles. I wasn't supposed to wear anything Egyptian, but any Greek woman could easily have bought this necklace in the market as a souvenir of her travels.

Finally, I tucked Maia's vial at the bottom of the chest.

I dozed on the bed. When I woke, it was dark. Antinous sat at the wooden table, concentrating on an open scroll in the light of a single oil lamp.

"What are you reading?" I asked idly from the shadows.

"It is the treatise by Thales that introduced Egyptian geometry to Greece." He sounded enthusiastic; there was a new shine to his eyes.

Thank you, Hermes, for my years with math tutors. How long ago did Hermes make his plans? Since my birth? Since before?

"What is your opinion of Pythagoras and his postulates on deductive reasoning?" I asked.

"Pythagoras takes Thales to new levels," Antinous answered quite passionately. "He hypothesizes that mathematics is the key to the cosmos."

He looked directly in the direction of my voice. I felt the first contact.

"Pythagoras sees numbers in everything," he added.

He sat in a halo of light in the quiet cabin. The lamp sputtered. The night was silent except for the sea washing against the hull, carrying us west along the coast of Africa to Greek Libya. Even the seagulls slept.

I enjoyed that we spoke Greek together. It's a lilting tongue that tickles the ears with vowels. No guttural sounds or hiccups, it's all music and poetry, easy to modulate—easy to insinuate other meaning.

"I regret I did not meet Pythagoras while in Saïs." My voice, resonating like the low notes of a lyre, filled the small cabin with promise.

His eyelids flickered. The glow of the oil lamp lighted his face, casting delicate shadows on perfect bones.

"Pythagoras would enjoy your intellect, Isidora. He teaches that men and women are equal."

Isidora. My new name. I took his use of it as a sign that we could start anew.

Antinous took a sharp intake of air when I came into the ring of light. His pupils were large and black; all trace of blue had disappeared.

The cut of my gown was loose, but designed to fall on the curves of the body, along the rise of my breasts and the slope of my hips. The hormones of early pregnancy were rounding out angles. I was fast becoming a curvaceous Greek.

He sat sideways to the table. His long legs with tight loins and rounded calves were stretched out and crossed at the ankles. The fabric of his *chiton* draped on his muscled thighs. His body was indeed perfect, exactly proportional, every muscle toned. He must have wrestled all his life.

I glided smoothly and silently toward him. When I leaned over him to ease the scroll from his hands, my swollen breasts pulled at the yellow linen. My nipples rose.

Ever so slowly, never taking my eyes from his, I pulled my gown past my knees and straddled him. My soft loins squeezed his hard thighs.

Antinous was so still, he might have been a statue. He didn't blink; he didn't breathe. I placed my palms on his chest. His muscles were so tense, his skin so smooth, he even felt like marble.

But heat rose off him; the tang of salt mixed with his strong scent of male. I could feel the warmth of the sun in his flesh.

In one day at sea, his skin had turned golden in the way of fair Greeks who reflect the sun. His eyes were transfixed on my face. Would he reject me tonight as he did in the tunnel?

"Husband," I whispered, and leaned to brush my lips against his.

I had no warning. He was on his feet in one movement, his hands on my buttocks, my legs straddling his thighs. The chair crashed to the floor. The table rocked. I expected the lamp to fall and splatter oil and fire on the carpets.

Antinous drove me straight to the wall. It happened so fast, I could only throw my arms around his neck and hang on. His mouth was on mine and his tongue down my throat. My head slammed against the cedar paneling. He held me with one hand and dragged my caftan up past my waist with the other. Then he jerked his loincloth off and flung it across the room.

He plunged into me and pounded me, both hands back on my buttocks. The rough edges of the wood paneling scraped my back as he banged me and banged me against the wall. He must have rocked the whole ship.

When he took his mouth from mine and allowed me to breathe, I used my cheek to force him to turn his head, and then one hand to hold him there. I put my wet tongue in his ear and blew and sucked gently, enough to torment, but not enough to damage.

He went wild and climaxed with a jolt that wracked his whole body. Collapsing against me, he pressed me into the wall, his forehead on the cedar close to my ear, his breath coming in gulps. He never loosened his grip. I was sure the flesh of my buttocks would forever show an imprint of his fingers.

His melon biceps bulged when he walked us to the bed, my thighs squeezing his thighs, his manhood still inside me. Then he tossed me down and flipped me over in one swift movement, dragging me up on my hands and knees. He ripped the Greek wig away and yanked the linen gown over my head. I heard seams tear.

Not possible, but he was iron-hard again. He thrust into me, holding my hips in both hands and lifting me up and into him. My face buried in the blankets, I reached to grab the back of his thighs and hold on. The two of us rocked with such force, the joint where the bed met the wall creaked with strain.

He pulled out of me and rolled me to my back. His tongue was deep in my mouth at the moment he entered me again. I wrapped my thighs around his waist, locked my ankles, and lay back, eyes closed, surrendering to pleasure.

My arms over my head, stretched out on the bed, palms up, I let him ravage me. He was tireless. He pounded and pounded until I feared the bones in my pelvis would separate. But I didn't stop him. We were both drenched in sweat.

Like a master choreographer, he turned us on our sides and pulled my hips into the curve of his belly, sliding again into my wet. I lay limp and helpless as a rag doll.

His hands massaged my tender, engorged breasts; I had a wild vision of milk spewing forth. He rolled my nipples aflame from new hormones between his thumb and finger, relentlessly, not quite rough, not aimed to hurt me, but not gently. I cried out in pain, but put his hands back when he stopped. I'd never felt such raw sensitivity. Agony and ecstasy in the same moment.

I gasped when he slid his finger onto my engorged bud and rotated hard. Moans reverberated through my chest and vibrated in my throat. My bud flowered. My womb contracted and contracted. The muscles in my vagina sucked his hardness.

Antinous cried out and went rigid, shuddering twice, then a third time.

We lay panting, completely spent, sweat glistening on our bare skin in spite of the cool sea night, my full breast filling his warm palm. I nestled my hips against his flat stomach and felt his lips cool on my bare scalp, his breath warm on my skin.

When he rolled over to his back, he turned me with him, holding tightly, never letting go. I burrowed into his side, my shoulder in his armpit, my cheek on his chest. We didn't speak; the sound of our breathing was louder than the swells of the sea.

I thought only to shower him with affection, but when I eased on top of him and began nibbling his lips around their fullness and licking the deep cleft in his chin, he hardened again.

Three times! Oh, this Greek indeed had many talents!

Pushing myself up on bent knees, I straddled him, one leg on each side of his waist. Just at the moment my hand found his swollen manhood and guided him inside me, the flicker of twinkling sparkles flashed in the dark. Lamplight reflected off the fragile golden charms of my necklace. He reached up and touched a tiny rabbit.

Fecundity. I knew his character by that choice.

I laughed lightly, a sound like small golden bells, and rocked slowly back and forth, in a steady rhythm, milking him. He caught my tender breasts in his hands, gently squeezing their fullness before pulling them to his open lips.

There was no doubt in his eyes now.

"Antinous Thrice-Greatest, my husband, we are going to have a wonderful life."

I didn't need to summon the Power at all.

Chapter 26   Cleopatra's Barge

With Hermes' Red Mirror in the ship cabin, I simply decided to go home, and I was there. I didn't need Barb in Las Vegas to bring me back.

The first thing I saw was a note from Hector on the glass coffee table.

I was afraid to wake you up. Might have messed up your escape.
Hope you don't mind I took a shower and a beer.
You need more food in your fridge.
Te amo. Hector.

I drove into work late in the afternoon. I knew my boss Ed would be furious about my missing days. His face went beet red when he saw me. Smoke poured out of his ears. He puffed up, eyes bulging, candidate for a stroke.

"Where the hell have you been? What's this shit about a sick friend? What kind of excuse is that? Whoever it is, they better be dead already."

I shut the door to Ed's office, closed my eyes for just a moment and summoned the Power. His eyes followed every movement as I slinked over to his desk and slithered onto the leather armrest of the chair opposite him.

Ed's red color paled to white. His mouth hung slightly open, lips slack. I could almost see his tongue. Smoke still steamed from his ears, but not from anger. I dialed it up a notch and leaned rather far forward, arching my back and twisting my shoulders just enough that the generous cleavage of my red V-neck sweater was front and center.

"Ed, I was thinking that I should work more from home," I oozed. "I get a lot more done."

I lowered my voice to a hush and wet my lips with the tip of my tongue.

"You wouldn't have a problem with that, Ed, would you? We could meet a couple of times a week, maybe over drinks? You know, just to touch base."

Easing down into the chair, I crossed one long leg slowly over the other, raising it just a tad too high so Ed couldn't help but catch a glimpse of my inner thigh. Black boots hugged my calves to the knees. From there to the hem of my short leather skirt was smooth skin—lots of it.

I had taken a tip from Isis and drawn thick dark lines along my lashes; emerald eyeshadow highlighted the deep jade of my eyes. My brazen gaze was direct and full of promise.

"What do you think, Ed? Do you think we can work something out?"

I had just walked in the front door and poured myself a glass of Chardonnay when my cell buzzed. I didn't recognize the number but broke my own rule and answered anyway.

"Isis, this is Rasheed."

Just the sound of his voice, exactly like River God's, paralyzed me. The air in the room crushed in and then sucked outward. My brain felt like a down pillow.

"Isis, are you there?"

"Yes, I'm here. I'm just a little stunned."

"Why?"

Could he really be that unaware of the effect he had on me?

"I didn't think I would hear from you again."

"Why would you think that?"

He sounded genuinely surprised. He saw no problem with coming and going in my life as he pleased. He took his *we have known each before, and we will know each other again* a bit too literally. At least I had enough pride not to agree right away.

"You just left," I accused him. "No forwarding address. Remember?"

"I told you how it has to be," he said quietly. "There are things you can't know. It's safer this way."

Safe from what? But I didn't ask. Maybe I didn't want to know.

"Well, I'm here now, Isis. I want to see you."

Of course, I knew from the moment I first heard his voice that I'd do anything to feel his touch again.

"Isis?"

"Yes?"

"Meet me. Please."

Please. That was a start. What I really wanted was for him to beg—like I'd begged on his ship. I waited. Wherever he was, it was quiet. The silence on the phone was deafening.

"Isis, what's going on? I want you, and I know that you want me. Why are you playing games?"

My game was to see how far I could push, but I lost my nerve when he turned Commander.

"Isis. We don't have time to waste. Meet me at Caesar's Palace. I'll get a suite. You can wait for me there."

I was afraid his next words might be goodbye. Besides, it was ridiculous to blame Rasheed for something River God did 2500 years ago. And Rasheed wasn't going to beg. I gave in just like I knew I would. But I was fresh from my conquest of Ed. I wasn't without power.

"I'm not going to wait in your room like some kind of call girl."

I don't think Rasheed knew what to say because he didn't say anything.

"And do you plan on disappearing when you're finished with me? Like you did at the Wynn?"

I heard him take a deep breath through his mouth, as if summoning patience.

"Okay, Isis. What do you want?" His tone was flat with more than a hint of irritation. "Do you want to meet in a restaurant? Do you want to meet me at a bar? Just tell me, Isis."

I sensed he found me unreasonable but had decided it was part of a package deal he had to put up with.

"I'll meet you at Cleopatra's Barge." I thought I was pretty clever myself.

Rasheed laughed, the first time I ever heard him—or River God—laugh.

"Cleopatra's Barge. Perfect! About 9?" His tone was light, almost playful for a moment before he reverted to his normal intensity.

"I may be late," he warned. "You know how these things are."

"Sure, Rasheed, I know how these things are. I'll be at the bar."

"And Isis, I only have tonight."

"It's okay. I'll wait for you."

I'd wait for him forever. I was pretty sure he knew it.

I chose a sleeveless red satin dress that hugged my bust, waist and hips. Flesh-toned, sheer stockings ended in scarlet stilettos with thin ankle straps. I even wore the red and black garters from the night of the Wynn. I topped it all off with a white mink that cost me $600 in my favorite vintage shop. I didn't hold anything back.

The traffic on the Strip at this hour would be a nightmare. I took Koval and turned left on Sands, driving past the Wynn with its bittersweet memories of Rasheed in the penthouse suite with stunning view. I used the back entrance to Caesar's, the one only cab drivers know.

A blond valet with nice shoulders took my keys, and I stepped out—long legs, red satin, white BMW. The look in his eyes told me everything I needed to know. *Bring it on, Rasheed.*

It was early for Vegas. No one else sat at the bar. I eased onto a padded barstool and ordered a Plymouth martini, up with an olive. I had already finished half of it and no sign of Rasheed. I checked my cell again. The only message was from Barb asking me to meet her at the Stirling Club.

"I'm at Caesar's—waiting for Rasheed." I said it very cool, as if meeting him was a common occurrence.

"Rasheed! Why didn't you tell me?"

"I was afraid I would jinx it. Besides, I know you don't like him."

"Don't let him jerk you around."

Actually Barb, I'm looking forward to him doing whatever he wants.

"And it's not that I can't see he's hot. He's just a little too unavailable for my taste."

"I'll call you tomorrow, Barb, and tell you all about it."

I put my phone down beside my martini glass. A man took the stool next to me, but I didn't look up.

"Looks like you're expecting someone," he said politely. "May I buy you a drink while you wait?"

I nearly knocked over my glass when I heard his voice. Antinous had traded his Greek *chiton* for a powder-blue oxford cloth shirt. He had the clean cut, preppy look of a Brooks Brothers ad. His face was golden tan except for the white around his eyes, like a pair of goggles. He must be a skier.

His hair was a mass of shiny curls. The same deep cleft split his chin. Gorgeous as ever, he outshone any of the statues at Caesar's.

"My name's Tony." He held out his hand for me to shake.

I looked at his outstretched hand and remembered how it gripped my butt so hard on the Phoenician ship that I bruised. For an awkward moment, his hand hung suspended in the narrow space between us, and then he put it on the bar.

"Excuse me if I was out of line," he apologized. He shifted his weight away from me. He didn't recognize me at all.

"I'd love another martini," I said with a warm smile. "I just wanted to make sure you weren't a salesman."

"You can tell I'm not a salesman?"

"Believe me, I can tell."

I didn't embarrass him by saying I also could see he wasn't local; he had that out-of-towner expectant look, *This is Vegas. Anything can happen.*

The bartender put two icy Plymouth martinis with plump olives in front of us.

Tony was so beautiful, it was criminal he was male. I knew a lot of women who paid a fortune to have blond-streaked curls like his. I almost regretted I was meeting Rasheed. I'd love to see if this Tony was as ferocious a lover as Antinous.

"I'm from New Jersey," he offered without my asking.

"New Jersey?" The thought of Antinous ending up in New Jersey saddened me a little.

"Well, from Princeton to be exact."

That was more like it. He had to be the best looking professor in the Ivy League. His preppy clothes didn't hide his muscles at all. He had the same wrestler's thighs and powerful arms that had crushed me on the ship.

"What about you?" he asked.

"I live here."

"You *live* in Las Vegas?"

I don't know why people are always so surprised when I say that; there are 2 million others like me.

"Living here is like living anywhere, except there's more to do when you go out. And I get to dress up. I like wearing my high heels."

I probably shouldn't have added the last part; the male in Tony couldn't resist looking the length of my red satin dress all the way to those heels. I had no trouble imagining him rip my clothes off as he drove me to the wall of Cleopatra's Barge.

That's when Rasheed came down the concourse. I could spot him in a crowd of a thousand. Like a lioness in heat, I sniffed his pheromones from afar.

He walked with a group of tough-looking men in pricey business suits. Some scanned the room while the others talked. His two bodyguards, Marcos and Gamel, walked close by him.

"It was great talking to you, Tony, but I see my date."

"Sure, I understand. Here's my card. If you're ever in Princeton, look me up. It's quiet there, but I know a couple of places to get a good martini."

He paused for a second as if waiting for me to say something. "You never told me your name."

I only hesitated a moment before answering, "It's...uh...Isis."

"Isis? Isn't that the name of an Egyptian goddess?" Something sparked in his eyes. "It seems like I knew an Isis once, but I can't remember where."

I put his card in my bag.

Rasheed walked up behind me, put one hand on my shoulder and moved my hair away with the other. He touched his lips to the trigger point on my neck, not a real kiss, just a fleeting brush that burned on. He breathed in my scent like an animal before mating. The heat from his hand seared my skin through the satin.

He took the empty stool on my other side and faced me. His legs were spread open; his knee pressed into my calf.

"You look good enough to eat," he breathed in my ear.

I thought the same thing about the bulge between his thighs.

His chiseled lips wouldn't reject me tonight. I wondered if there existed a Hathor Power for men. I wanted to jump him right there at the bar.

"Let's have dinner in the room." He was cheerful for Rasheed, almost buoyant. His eyes, warm with affection, glowed like polished jade.

But then his face hardened. His skin actually darkened. He had seen Tony. No doubt about him recognizing the Greek. Rasheed's face took on the black rage of the night below deck on River God's ship.

I put my hand on the inside of his thigh. High up, to get his attention.

"Rasheed, he doesn't know. Trust me. He has no idea."

He scared me. I didn't like the way he looked at Tony. I slid down from the stool and took his hands. I leaned into him, between his open legs, pressing against his bulge. My breasts were soft and full against his hard chest.

"Let's go up to the suite," I breathed in his ear.

It was like I wasn't there. Rasheed glared at Tony with cold hatred in his eyes, the warm jade frozen to green ice. Then Marcos the bodyguard appeared and spoke so low that, close as I was, I couldn't hear what he said. Rasheed nodded, but still glared at Tony who was walking away.

For one wild crazy instant, I thought that Rasheed might be ordering a hit on him.

Taking me by the arm, he guided me across the empty dance floor, saying, "Why don't you take a seat in a booth over here? I'll just be a few minutes."

We passed a group of hard-looking men seated around a table, and I flashed on mafia bosses deciding who will live and who will die. They stopped talking. I felt their eyes following us.

Rasheed helped me into a red leather booth and then leaned down and kissed me on the lips in a way that said, *This woman belongs to me.*

Everything with Rasheed has to be mysterious and high drama.

Bodyguards milled around with no attempt to be inconspicuous. This was Caesar's Palace; the mob had been coming here since the days of the Rat Pack.

Tony's card read 'Anthony Callis, Ph.D., Director of Cosmological Research, Institute for Advanced Study, Princeton NJ.'

He was legit. It fit my sense of cosmic order that Antinous the mathematician was reborn as Tony the astronomer or cosmologist, or whatever the difference was. I wondered if he were married, had kids. I wondered about his life with Isis—Isidora—in Greece. I wondered about the General's child.

A waiter set a glass of champagne in front of me at the same time a large man slid into the booth on the opposite bench. He moved fast and sat there before I looked up.

He had a salon haircut, styled back on the sides with neck hair too long for an American. He was clean-shaven, but I would have known him anywhere. His massive chest and biceps stretched the expensive Italian-looking suit. I visualized the thickness of his thighs bulging the cashmere of his pants.

My eyes fixed on the green silk tie with arabesque pattern at his throat. Dark red blood began to bubble above the knot as I stared.

"Hello, Ishtar. It has been a long time."

He called me by the name he'd given me in his Persian tent in the desert.

I couldn't avoid his eyes any longer. I took a deep breath and then exhaled.

"Hello, General."

Chapter 27 Full Circle

Rasheed arrived at my side in seconds. I didn't need to look at him to know his mood. His energy field was like the strobe of a pulsar.

The General nodded his massive head, a smug smile on his face.

"Your lady friend is most charming, Rasheed. I envy you."

They knew each other! The shock of it slammed me. But it was in this life, not the other. River God and the General never met in the desert.

"We should go now." Rasheed took hold of my upper arm.

"Wait. Have a drink with me, Rasheed. You and your lovely friend."

The General's tone sounded friendly, but it was clear he expected us to stay.

"Let us celebrate."

The muscles in Rasheed's jaw clenched, but he didn't say no.

"Let us celebrate relationships: past, present and future," the General said, looking directly at me.

Rasheed nudged me, and I slid over. We sat so close our arms and thighs touched. As if by magic, a bottle of *Cristal* arrived with more flutes.

The hypnotic white noise of slot machines played in the background. Herds of tourists streamed past. The show at the

Coliseum finished, and the crowd poured out.

Rasheed fixed his unblinking, hard, glittery eyes on the General.

"I sense that your beautiful friend and I have met before."

The General sipped his champagne and smiled benignly.

I couldn't help my eyes widening. Surely the General wouldn't bring up what happened between us, not in front of Rasheed. If Rasheed realized this was the Persian who had tasted me, if he had the slightest hint of my ride on the comet, it would take more than bodyguards to pull him off.

"You have the most stunning eyes," the General continued, nodding his massive head at me in approval. "I have always had a weakness for emerald eyes like yours. They have been my downfall on more than one occasion."

He enjoyed himself, happily watching me squirm, waving a red cape in Rasheed's face. But it was the bull goading the matador.

Electric shocks ran from Rasheed's body into mine.

"Rasheed and I are business partners, did you know that, *bella*? You must find that a fascinating turn of events."

The General's tone was far too intimate. Did he want a war right here at Caesar's Palace?

The impact of his words on Rasheed was obvious. He hadn't spoken; he barely breathed. He was like the cobra in the desert, eyes fixed, head almost swaying. I had to do something before he uncoiled and struck at the General's throat.

"What kind of business are you in?" I tried to sound polite and disinterested.

"The world is a dangerous place, *ma bella*. Everyone feels they must protect themselves. I help them do that. I am—what might you call it?—a broker of deals."

He toyed with me. Did he use that vague, taunting tone just to annoy? He succeeded.

"What is it exactly that you broker? Or is it a secret? Or maybe it's secrets that you broker?"

He threw back his head and laughed. It was the same laugh as in the tent when I accused him of not being a man of his word. Rasheed couldn't help but notice the familiarity between us.

The General leaned over the table, closer to me.

"You've got guts, I like that. But then I've always liked that about you, Ishtar."

Rasheed turned his face to me, icy eyes narrowed with suspicion and distrust. I read his thoughts. *She didn't tell me about her plan with the Greek. What other silent lies has she told?*

The General stood out of the booth. I didn't look at him; I couldn't look away from Rasheed's accusing eyes. I found myself wishing that he had River God's black eyes, convincing myself that the glint of hard obsidian would be easier to bear than this cold green glass.

"*Á vedeci, bella.* It was my pleasure to see you again. I am sure this is not the last time we will run into each other."

He walked away, his bodyguards around him, devastation in his wake.

The bubbles in my glass rose from bottom to top in a continuous stream. I hadn't even tasted the champagne. I was afraid to look down at my dress, afraid there would be a lurid stain of bright blood gushing from my slashed throat.

Rasheed's aura had gone black, and his eyelid twitched in a spasm. He frightened me; his dark jealousy twisted his mind and shut off his heart. I was losing him. He retreated as fast as one of Tony's galaxies hurtling through space. The heat of his arm cooled as we sat.

I would gladly have lied, but my mind was blank. I couldn't explain away the General. He had gotten his revenge without raising a hand.

Rasheed's frigid face formed the same harsh angles as below deck on River God's ship, but minus the fury. I thought his face would shatter with one flick of my finger. He always could turn his feelings from hot to cold like a shower faucet.

"I'm going home now." I said it quite simply without much

emotion in my voice.

But as hard as I tried, I couldn't stop my eyes from filling with tears. My three-inch heels put me on level with his once lush mouth. It seemed impossible that those hard lips had pleasured me and made my soul sing. I wanted to kiss him, to warm him from stone to man, but his granite mouth was cold.

Just like the night below deck, there would be no melting Rasheed. He refused to look at me, trying once more to make me a non-person. I didn't bother to summon the Power.

"Maybe you'll call me when you can let go of the past," I told him. I didn't try to hide my sadness and regret.

Then I turned and walked away. He didn't stop me. He hadn't said one word at all since he first came to my booth and faced the General.

I don't remember the drive home. Even the next morning, my mind sped but went nowhere. I kept seeing faces, as they looked in Egypt, as they looked now, changing back and forth. There seemed to be no rules about who remembered what. I was a stranger to Tony, but Rasheed knew him instantly. Hector had seen me as Isis the moment we met at Carla's party.

I sensed the General knew much more than any of us. His words—without actually saying anything at all—severed Rasheed from me with the precision of a surgeon.

Barb called twice before I had the courage to answer. But instead of her usual "I told you so," she was sympathetic and caring.

"I'm sorry. I really am. I know this guy has a hold on you that just won't let go."

"Well, I'm pretty sure we can count on it being over. There's no reaching him when he's like this."

"You know, I was thinking," Barb said. "If Hector can go through the mirror, then anyone could, right?"

"I suppose so...I don't really know," I answered cautiously. Where was Barb going with this?

"My love life's not all that great," she said. "And you did come back with three gorgeous men."

I called Hector as soon as I got off the phone with Barb. Half an hour later, he picked me up in his white Range Rover. He wore faded tight jeans with a yellow polo shirt and lizard cowboy boots. A worn bomber jacket lay on the back seat.

"*Á donde vamos?*" he asked with his blazing white smile. "Your wish is my command."

He looked so like Hetmus-hor in that moment, the confident Hetmus on the morning of the hunt, before he lost me in the sandstorm and everything went wrong.

"You decide. I just needed company."

What I really meant was that I needed to be with someone who wanted me.

He smiled in a way that said he was pleased, but he didn't comment. I stared out the huge windows of the Range Rover and told myself Rasheed didn't deserve me.

"You have many beautiful things in your home. *Muy impresionante.*"

I rarely brought men back to my condo, but when I did, they weren't much interested in the furniture.

"Show me where you find such treasures in Las Vegas."

"Seriously? Most men don't like shopping."

"I am not most men."

He was certainly not most men. I'd never believed in the G-Spot until Hector, but he'd made me a believer.

I keyed the address into the GPS. The traffic thinned as we moved along Flamingo away from the Strip.

"You're not married, are you?" I asked suddenly.

I'd never asked Rasheed if he were married. I'd never asked Rasheed anything.

"No, Isis, I am not married. I have been waiting for you."

"I'm not very good at commitments either," I answered.

He locked eyes with me for a just a second.

"We will have to work on that," he said.

His look told me that working with Hector could be very pleasurable indeed. I studied his profile with strong Latin nose and head of chestnut waves combed back from his brow. His big hands with those long fingers that went straight to the Spot gripped the wheel in a relaxed, self-assured way.

He had crossed through the Red Mirror for me. I doubted Rasheed would do that.

"What's Argentina like?" I rather suddenly was interested in exploring my options.

"Buenos Aires is full of life, like Las Vegas. But I grew up on an *estancia*, a ranch."

The ranch accounted for his ease in the cowboy boots. And those powerful thighs. I imagined his long legs squeezing the horse's sides as he twisted and dipped in the saddle.

"So, what is it that you actually *do*? I mean, besides play polo."

"I used to chase all beautiful women. Now I chase only you."

Hector, the man who never struggled for anything, was back in his teasing mode.

"Are you telling me you're a playboy?"

"I prefer to think of myself as a man, not a boy."

We pulled into the parking lot of the antique mall on Eastern. Hector followed me down the aisles filled with armor suits, models of sailing ships, neon beer signs and embroidered Spanish shawls.

"Here's where I found the Red Mirror. It was just over there, against the Chinese screen."

No one was in the stall at the end of the maze, just like the first afternoon I saw the Red Mirror and just like the day I bought it.

Hector pulled me back into him, slid his hand between my thighs, and lifting me off the ground like I weighed nothing, carried me behind the yellow-flowered screen. He kissed my neck and my throat and nibbled at my ear. I gyrated my hips into his groin and whimpered while he stroked my breasts.

"I have wanted to do that since you first got in the car," he breathed into my neck as he turned me around.

His tongue was first deep in my throat and then in my ear. All the while his big hand with his strong cowboy fingers was between my legs. I was alive at his touch even through the thick denim.

He bent me slightly backwards and put his mouth on my sweater, suckling me through the wool. My hair swung in the air as I arched my back. Only the security camera stopped me from lifting my top. His strong hands, firm and commanding, but without a trace of roughness, pressed on my stomach and down the inside of my loin.

The Spot burned like fire. Just the memory of his fingers there sent electric shocks through my buttocks, down my thighs and deep into my womb.

"You are so desirable, Isis. I want to touch you forever."

He stroked my breasts and the line of my hips. He suckled more. The pink of my sweater turned red where his mouth had been.

Iron fingers massaged me through my jeans. I was so wet I was sure there would be a stain. He eased down the zipper at the same time he leaned me back into a bookshelf. His fingers slid under my panties. I spread my legs to a V.

A vase fell first. Hector grabbed it in midair. But the bookcase kept swaying and when I reached back to steady it, I knocked a shelf loose, and a stack of dusty books, then something heavy, fell to the floor.

We both stared at the mess in horror and then at each other. Hector grinned.

"Look what you do to me," he said and kissed me lightly on the lips.

I don't think the security camera worked, because no one came running.

"Nothing's broken that I can see, so we're saved," I said.

Then I thought, it probably wouldn't matter to Hector. He'd just write a check. He wouldn't even think of cleaning up.

But Hector bent to the floor and picked up a canvas-wrapped

packet about the size of a large, thick atlas. I recognized the size and shape immediately. Luckily it had fallen last and landed on a soft pile of books. He turned the crumbling fabric back, and a glint of shiny green glass shimmered in the fluorescent light.

"This is Greek script," he said. "It looks really old."

I could tell by his voice that he was a little in awe.

The hard glassy surface was covered with neat rows of hand-etched Greek letters. They formed words so familiar I could have been reading from today's newspaper.

the following to be the truth…

The Emerald Tablet.

I looked around the stall, half expecting Hermes Trismegistus to be there. *I have manifested the Emerald Tablet and I have manifested you.*

My hands trembled when Hector handed me the Tablet. It must have been here all along, waiting for me to find it. But I no longer believed that I ever found anything, but rather that fate found me.

Hermes Thrice-Greatest wasn't finished; I wasn't finished. The circle of souls was not finished.

Hector slid his hand around my waist and pulled me back into him, but not hot with passion this time. His other hand reached across my breasts and around my shoulder to wrap me in his arms. He held me close but not tight. I could fly away and still come back to rest.

Leaning my head on his chest, letting him carry my weight, I relaxed into the cocoon of his body. Safe. Hector always made me feel safe.

For a moment, I was tempted to tell him all about the Emerald Tablet. He had traveled through the Red Mirror for me. He deserved to know.

But Hermes Trismegistus had been clear. *You are the chosen one, my daughter. It is your destiny to protect the Tablet.*

"This tablet is something very special, Hector." I said cautiously. "More special than you could ever imagine."

"Then you must have it. It is yours."

He grinned his broad confident smile; I could see how much pleasure it gave him to please me. Being with him when he smiled was like watching Ra Rising.

When he saw how serious I was, he took my chin in his fingers and looked me deep in the eyes. His were the warmest of browns freckled with those reddish specks that picked up the highlights of his chestnut hair.

"Everything is yours, Isis, if you just let me give it to you."

I was tempted. Oh, how I was tempted. But did I really need Hector to give me what I wanted?

Now that I had the Emerald Tablet, couldn't I manifest everything myself? Couldn't I also have River God?

Cast of Characters

Isis. (*Eye sis*) Isenkhebe Nefrusobek (*EE sin ke bay Ne fru sew beck*), Ishtar (*Ish tar*) [*Persian*], Isidora *Ee see do ra* [*Greek*]

Her four lovers (in order of appearance)
River God. Egyptian Commander. Rasheed (*Ra sheed*)
Hetmus-hor. (*Het-moose-hor*) Egyptian Master of Hunt. Hector
General Sher. (*Cher*) Persian general. The General
Antinous. (*An te no us*) Greek mathematician. Tony

Rest of cast (in alphabetical order)
Aisha. (*Eye sha*) The Vegas cat.
Ankh-hor. (*Onk-hor*) Nobleman and father of Hetmus.
Barb. Very Best Friend. Cambyses. (*Kam boo sees*) King of Persia.
Carla. Friend.
Ed. Boss.
Goliath. Isis' Nubian slave.
Hermes Trismegistus. (*Err mees Tris me gis tus*) Emerald Tablet Creator & Isis' father.
Maia. (*My ah*) Handmaiden to Isis.
Pehtes. (*Pay tes*) The Egyptian cat.
Psamtik. (*Sam tick*) Crown Prince of Egypt.
Qeb-ha. (*Keb ha*) Eunuch priest.
Sit-hathor. (*Sit ha thor*) High Priestess & mother of Isis.
The Scribe. The Crown Prince's partner.

About the author

Author website: www.SandraGore.com

Born with wanderlust, forever living in a fantasy world, Sandra Gore escaped the prairies of Kansas to follow the yellow brick road on an odyssey that took her to Europe, Africa, Latin America and the Middle East.

Starting with a one way ticket to Iceland, Sandra returned with a Viking husband, an art degree and speaking five languages.

She drew on her love of travel, classical history, languages, mysticism, food, shopping and romance to create her first novels of the *Red Mirror Series*: **The Red Mirror** and **The Emerald Tablet**. Sandra is currently working on **The Black Scroll**.

She has also written the self-help **Sex and the Zen of Shopping**: *How to Live Rich by Shopping Smart* and contributed memoir pieces to three **Life Choices** anthologies.

Her long-term project is a cookbook of her own recipes plus those of talented, cooking friends around the globe.

Sandra and her husband have a grown daughter and son and divide their time between a California beach house and a Las Vegas condo.

Sandra's books

If the story of Isis intrigues you, and you would fancy a more intricate version with richer sub-plots, a couple more characters, and a mini-encyclopedia of Egyptology, check out the Red Mirror Series.

Red Mirror Series ~ *One life is not enough*
S.L. Gore
Published by Tajine Publishing in print and eVersion

The Red Mirror (Book One)
- Pharaonic Egypt, 525 BC
The Emerald Tablet (Book Two)
- Greek Egypt, 215 BC
The Black Scroll (Book Three)
- Roman North Africa, 130 AD

Isis *Erotica*
Published by Tajine Publishing in print and eVersion

Isis Beach Read
Published by Tajine Publishing in print and eVersion

Sex and the Zen of Shopping: Live Rich by Shopping Smart
Sandra Gore Nielsen
Published by Tajine Publishing

Life Choices Anthologies
Published by Turning Point International
Navigating Difficult Paths: "A True Love Story"
Pursuing Your Passion: "The Muses Whisper"
It's Never Too Late: "Road to Vegas"

Tajine Publishing
2550 E Desert Inn Rd, #443
Las Vegas, NV 89121

tajinepublishing@gmail.com
702-279-6556